"Am I dead?"

"No, Mr. Cassidy," Norah answered with a reassuring smile. Obviously the medication was continuing to block out the pain; otherwise he'd know exactly how alive he was.

"Should be," he whispered, as though speaking demanded a real effort.

"You're a very lucky man, Mr. Cassidy. You survived a plane crash."

He attempted a grin but didn't quite succeed. "Who are you? My fairy godmother?"

"Not quite. I'm Norah Bloomfield, Valerie's sister. And I'm a nurse. I was on duty when they brought you in last night."

"Unusual uniform." He gestured weakly at her pale rose, floor-length gown.

Once again, Norah found herself smiling. "I was in my sister's wedding this afternoon."

"So Valerie decided to go through with it after all, did she?"

"Yes."

Silence filled the room.

Dear Reader,

I'm thrilled and excited that you're reading the ORCHARD VALLEY trilogy. These three books—*Valerie, Stephanie* and *Norah*—come straight from my heart.

I was born and raised in Yakima, Washington, which is often referred to as the apple capital of the world. Huge orchards spread out across the Yakima Valley, and the scent of flowering apple trees fills the air each spring. How well I remember their beauty—and the dread of a late-spring freeze!

I've loosely based Orchard Valley on Yakima and on the small town of Port Orchard, where my husband and I moved several years ago to raise our family. Although I've situated Orchard Valley in Oregon, it could be any small town, anywhere in the United States or Canada. Any small town where there's a sense of community, where people help each other, where neighbors become friends. I hope I've succeeded in capturing that wonderful small-town feeling.

The sisters in these three books are reunited because of a family crisis. There's nothing like the threat of losing someone we love to help us recognize our real values and appreciate our families, our roots. I hope that (like me!) you'll weep with Valerie as she discovers what really matters in life and that you'll sympathize with Stephanie as she deals with her past. And I'm sure you'll cheer with Norah as she meets her match!

I'd be delighted to learn your reactions to the ORCHARD VALLEY trilogy. (In fact, I *always* love hearing from my readers!) You can write to me at P.O. Box 1458, Port Orchard, Washington 98366.

Sincerely,

Debbie Macomber

NORAH
Debbie Macomber

Harlequin Books

TORONTO • NEW YORK • LONDON
AMSTERDAM • PARIS • SYDNEY • HAMBURG
STOCKHOLM • ATHENS • TOKYO • MILAN
MADRID • WARSAW • BUDAPEST • AUCKLAND

To Dorothy Tharp
in appreciation for her many talents

ISBN 0-373-03244-7

Harlequin Romance first edition January 1993

NORAH

CHAPTER ONE

THIS COWBOY was too young to die!

Norah Bloomfield stared down at the unconscious face of the man in Orchard Valley Hospital's emergency room. He was suffering from shock, internal injuries and a compound fracture of the right fibula. Yet he was probably the luckiest man she'd ever known. He'd survived.

The team of doctors worked vigorously over him, doing everything humanly possible to keep him alive. Although she was busy performing her own role in this drama, Norah was curious. It wasn't every day a man literally fell out of the sky into their backyard. Whoever he was, he'd been involved in a plane accident. From what she heard when they'd rushed him in, he'd made a gallant effort to land the single-engine Cessna in a wheatfield, but the plane's wing tip had caught the ground, catapulting it into a series of cartwheels. That he'd managed to crawl out of the wreckage was a miracle all its own.

She tightened the blood-pressure cuff around his arm and called out the latest reading. Dr. Adamson, the physician in attendance, briskly instructed her to administer a shot.

Their patient was young, in his early thirties. And handsome in a rugged sort of way. Dark hair, chis-

eled jaw, stubborn as a mule from the looks of him.
His clothes, at least what was left of them, told her he
was probably a cowboy. She suspected he rode in the
rodeo circuit; successfully, too, if he was flying his own
plane.

Her gaze drifted down to his left hand. He wasn't
wearing a wedding ring and that eased her mind
somewhat. Norah hated the thought of a young wife
pacing the floor, anxiously waiting his arrival home.
Of course, that didn't necessarily mean he wasn't
married. A lot of men didn't wear wedding bands,
particularly if they worked with their hands. Too
dangerous.

His leg was badly broken, she noted, and once he
was stabilized, he'd be sent into surgery. She didn't
have a lot of experience with compound fractures, but
her guess was that he'd need to be in traction for the
next few weeks. A break as complex as this would take
months, possibly years, to heal properly.

Norah wasn't scheduled to work tonight, but had
been called in unexpectedly. She should have been
home, had *planned* to be home, preparing for her
oldest sister Valerie's wedding. Half of Orchard Valley would be in attendance—it was widely held to be
the event of the year. And five weeks after that, her
second sister, Steffie, would be marrying Charles
Tomaselli, in a much less formal ceremony.

There was definitely something in the air this summer, Norah mused, with both her sisters getting married so unexpectedly.

Love was what floated in the air, but it had apparently evaded Norah. There wasn't a single man in Orchard Valley who stirred her heart. Not one.

She was thrilled for her sisters, but at the same time she couldn't help feeling a bit envious. If any of the three could be described as "the marrying type," it was Norah. She was by far the most domestic and traditional. Ever since she was a teenager, Norah had assumed she'd be the first of the three sisters to marry, although she was the youngest. Valerie had hardly dated even in college, and Steffie was so impulsive and unpredictable that she'd never stood still long enough to get serious about anyone. Or so it had seemed...

Now both her sisters were marrying. And all this had happened within two short months. Only weeks ago Norah would have been shocked had anyone told her Valerie would become a wife. Her oldest sister was the dedicated career woman, working her way up the corporate ladder for CHIPS, a Texas-based computer software corporation. At least, that was what Valerie *had* been—until she flew home when their father suffered a serious heart attack. Before Norah was entirely aware it had happened, Valerie was head over heels in love with Dr. Colby Winston.

Norah never did understand what had led to their falling in love. Try as she might, she couldn't picture her sister as a wife. Valerie, who was so much like their father, was a dynamic businesswoman. She'd accepted the sales job with CHIPS and in less than four years had moved up into upper management. She was energetic, spirited and strong-willed. If her sister was going to fall in love, Norah couldn't understand how it could be with Dr. Winston. He was just as dedicated to his work, just as headstrong. To Norah's way of thinking, they had little in common except their love for each other. Watching them together had taught Norah a few things about love and commitment. They were both determined to make their marriage work, both willing to make compromises, to change and mediate their differences.

If Valerie was going to marry, Norah had always assumed it should be someone like Rowdy Cassidy, the owner of CHIPS. For months, Valerie's letters had been full of details about the maverick software developer. He'd taken Wall Street by storm with his innovative ideas, and had very soon come to dominate the field. Valerie greatly admired him. But she'd given up her position with CHIPS without so much as a second's regret. There were other jobs, she'd said, but only one Colby Winston. And if she had to choose, as Cassidy had forced her to do, then that choice was clear. But then Norah had never seen anyone more in love—unless it was Steffie.

Her second sister had arrived after a long, difficult trip, to be with their father and almost the same thing had happened. Suddenly, she and Charles Tomaselli, the Orchard Valley *Clarion*'s editor and now its publisher, had clashed. They'd been constantly at odds, but gradually that had changed. Not until much later did Norah learn that Charles was the reason Steffie had decided to study in Italy. Steffie had been wildly in love with him three years earlier. Norah wasn't entirely sure what had gone wrong back then, but whatever it was had sent Steffie fleeing. She guessed there'd been some sort of disagreement between them, but no one had bothered to explain it to her. Not that it mattered. What was important, though, was that Steffie and Charles had managed to patch things up and admit their true feelings for each other.

In typical Steffie fashion, her sister was planning a thoroughly untraditional wedding. The exchange of vows was to take place in the apple orchard, between the rows of trees with their weight of reddening apples. The reception would be held on the groomed front lawn; there would be musicians playing chamber music in the background. The wedding cake was to be a huge chocolate concoction.

So, within a few weeks of each other, her two sisters would be married. Unlike Valerie, Norah hadn't recently met a new and wonderful man. And unlike Steffie, she didn't have a secret love, someone she'd felt passionate about for years. Unless she counted Michael York. Norah figured she'd seen every movie he starred in ten times over. But it wasn't likely that a dashing actor was going to toss her over his shoulder and haul her away. A pity, really.

An hour later, Norah was washing up, preparing to head home. The cowboy, although listed in critical condition, had stabilized. He might not feel like it now, but he was damn lucky to be alive. The surgery on the right fibula would follow, but she wasn't sure exactly when.

Eager to leave the hospital and get home, Norah was on her way out the door when she heard someone mention the cowboy's name.

She stopped abruptly, nearly tripping in her astonishment. "Who did you say he is?" she demanded, turning back to her friends.

"According to the identification he carried, his name is Rowdy Cassidy."

"Rowdy!" Susan Parsons, another nurse, laughed. "It's a perfect name for him, isn't it? He looks rowdy.

Personally, I don't want to be around when he wakes up. Two dollars says he's going to have all the charm of an angry yellow jacket.''

Rowdy Cassidy. Norah took a deep breath. The man was Valerie's employer. Former employer, she amended. He must have been flying in for the wedding when the accident occurred.

Norah wasn't sure what she could do with the information. Valerie, who was cool as a watermelon on ice when it came to business dealings, was a nervous wreck over this wedding.

Love had taken Valerie Bloomfield by surprise and she hadn't recovered yet. Mentioning Rowdy's accident to her sister now didn't seem right; Valerie had enough on her mind without the additional worry. Yet it didn't seem fair to keep the truth from her, either.

Whom should she tell, then, Norah wondered on her way to the staff parking lot. Surely someone should know...

It was late, past midnight, when she entered the house. Although there were several lights on, she didn't see anyone around. The wedding was at noon, less than twelve hours away.

Secretly Norah had hoped her father might still be up, but she didn't really expect it. He went to bed early these days and slept late, his body regaining its strength after the physical ordeal of a heart attack and the subsequent life-saving surgery.

"Hi," Steffie said cheerfully. She hurried downstairs, cinching her robe at the waist as she walked. Her long dark hair was damp and fell arrow-straight to the middle of her back. "I wondered what time you'd be home."

Norah stared up at her, frowning in concentration. She'd discuss this with Steffie, see what her sister suggested.

"What happened?" Steffie asked, her voice urgent.

"There was a single-engine-plane crash." Norah hesitated. "Fortunately only one man was aboard."

"Did he survive?"

Norah nodded absently and worried her lower lip. "Is Valerie asleep?"

Steffie sighed. "Who knows? I'd never have believed Valerie would be this nervous before her wedding. Good grief, she's arranged multimillion-dollar business deals."

"Come in the kitchen with me," Norah said, glancing quickly up the staircase. She didn't want any possibility of Valerie hearing this.

"What is it?" Steffie asked as she followed her into the other room. Valerie's room was directly above, but there was little chance she'd overhear the conversation.

"The man who was involved in the plane accident..."

"Yes," Steffie prodded in a whisper.

"Is Rowdy Cassidy."

Looking stunned, Steffie pulled out a stool at the counter and sank down on it. "You're sure?"

"Positive. Apparently he was flying in for the wedding."

"More likely he intended to stop it," Steffie said sharply.

"Stop it? What do you mean?"

Steffie nodded, her look intense. "Well, you know that when Valerie talked to him about opening a branch on the West Coast, he was in favor of the idea, but he wanted someone else to head it up. He refused to give her the job, unless she could devote twenty-four hours a day to it. In other words, unless she chooses Rowdy Cassidy and her career over Colby and marriage. In fact, she seems to think he can persuade her to do just that."

"What a rotten way to act."

Steffie agreed. "Valerie was furious. She'd hoped to continue working for CHIPS after she's married. Rowdy demanded that she stay in Texas if she wanted to stay with CHIPS. She didn't have any alternative, so she submitted her resignation and announced she was marrying Colby. Apparently Rowdy didn't believe her—still doesn't. He seems to think it was some female ploy to get him to declare his love."

"I take it Mr. Cassidy doesn't know Valerie very well." Her sister was nothing if not direct, Norah mused with a small smile. Valerie would never stoop to orchestrating such a scene, or exploiting a man's feelings for her.

When Valerie first flew home after their father's heart attack, Norah had suspected her sister might have been attracted to her employer. In retrospect, she realized Valerie greatly admired and liked Rowdy, but wasn't in love with him. Her reactions to Colby made that abundantly clear.

"But what makes you think he wanted to stop the wedding?" Norah asked. If Rowdy did love her sister, he'd certainly waited until the last minute to do something about it.

"He phoned two days ago... I took the call," Steffie announced, a guilty expression crossing her face. "I didn't tell Valerie, but then how could I?"

"Tell her what, exactly?"

"That Rowdy asked her not to do anything... hasty until he'd had a chance to talk to her."

"Hasty?" Norah questioned.

"Like go through with the wedding."

"He had to be joking."

"I don't think so," Steffie said grimly. "He was dead serious. He claimed he had something important to say to her and that she should put everything on hold until he got here."

"You didn't tell Valerie?"

"No," Steffie returned, her gaze avoiding Norah's. "I know I should have, but when I told Dad—"

"Dad knows?"

"He didn't seem the least bit surprised, either." Steffie folded her arms around her middle and slowly shook her head. "He just smiled and then he said the most amazing thing."

"When hasn't he?" Norah muttered.

Steffie agreed with a quick smile.

"What was it this time?"

Steffie didn't answer right away. She stared down at the counter for a moment. Finally she glanced up, giving a baffled shrug. "That Rowdy was arriving right on schedule."

Norah found the statement equally puzzling. "Do you think Rowdy might have telephoned earlier and spoken to Dad?"

Once again Steffie shrugged. "Who knows?"

"But Dad seemed to think you shouldn't say anything to Valerie about Rowdy's call?" Norah pressed.

Steffie nodded. "Yeah. He says she's got enough to worry about. I couldn't agree more. As far as I'm concerned, Cassidy's had his chance. He accepted her resignation, which worked out fine since it gave Valerie more time to get everything organized for the wedding. From what she said recently, I think she might start doing some consulting. You know, help companies upgrade their computer systems."

"That's a great idea," Norah murmured. "Valerie's amazing."

"It isn't the wedding arrangements that have unsettled Val." Steffie spoke with the authority of one who knew. "It's being in love."

"Love," Norah repeated wistfully.

"Valerie's never been in love before, that's what threw her. Not the wedding plans or all the organizing or even this job situation."

"What amazes me the most," Norah said, thinking back over the past few weeks, "is how she immediately becomes composed whenever Colby's around."

"He's her emotional center," Steffie said knowingly. "Like Charles is mine. And—"

"Should I say anything to Val about Rowdy Cassidy?" Norah broke in.

"Sure," Steffie told her, "but my advice is to wait until after the ceremony."

Norah concurred, frowning a little.

"How badly was he injured?" Steffie asked.

"He's listed in critical condition and is scheduled for surgery on his leg. I think he'll be in traction for some time. He suffered some internal injuries, too, but they don't appear to be as serious as we first assumed."

"So he'll be pretty well out of it until after the wedding, anyway?"

"Oh, yes. He's not expected to fully regain consciousness until sometime tomorrow afternoon—if then."

"Then let's leave sleeping dogs lie, shall we?" Steffie suggested. "It's not like a visit from Valerie would do him any good—at least, not now."

"Are you sure we're doing the right thing?" Norah wasn't nearly as confident as her sister. Valerie had a right to know about her friend's accident.

"No," Steffie admitted after a moment. "I'm not at all sure. But I just can't see upsetting Valerie now, so close to the wedding. Especially when Cassidy isn't likely to know if she goes to see him, anyway."

Norah didn't know what to think or do. Apparently Rowdy cared enough for her sister to call her, and even to come to Orchard Valley. Perhaps he loved her. If that was the case, though, Rowdy Cassidy's love was too late.

JUST BEFORE NOON the next day, Norah was standing in the vestibule of the church, with the other members of the bride's party. Everyone—except Valerie—was giggling and jittery with nerves. Valerie no longer seemed nervous; now that the day she'd worried over and waited for had finally arrived, she was completely calm. Serene.

But Norah's head was spinning. This wasn't her first wedding by any means. She'd been a bridesmaid three

times before. Yet she'd never been more . . . excited.
That was the word for it. Excited and truly happy for
these two people she loved so much.

Although she'd never said anything to Valerie and
certainly never to Colby, she'd been a bit sweet on the
good doctor herself. Who wouldn't be? He was compassionate and gentle, but he also possessed a rugged
appeal. He wasn't one to walk away from a challenge. Loving Valerie had proved as much.

Norah's oldest sister had worked hard on her wedding preparations, and all her careful planning had
paid off. The church was lovely. Large bunches of
white gardenias decorated the end of each pew. The
sanctuary was filled with arrangements of white candles and a profusion of flowers—more gardenias,
white and yellow roses, pink apple blossoms.

The bridesmaids' dresses were in different pastels
and they carried flowers that complemented their
color. Norah's own pale-rose gown was set off by a
small bouquet of apple blossoms while Steffie, wearing a soft green gown, carried lemony rosebuds.

The fragrance of the flowers mingled and wafted
through the crowded church, carried by a warm breeze
that drifted through the open doors.

It was all so beautiful. The flowers, the ceremony,
the love between Valerie and Colby as they exchanged
their vows. Several times, Norah felt the tears gather
in her eyes. She hated being so sentimental, so maud-
lin, but she couldn't help herself. It was the most
touching, most *beautiful*, wedding she'd ever at-
tended.

Valerie was radiant. No other words could describe the kind of beauty that shone from her sister's face as she smiled up at her husband.

The reception, dinner and dance were to follow immediately afterward at the Orchard Valley Country Club. But first they were subjected to a series of photographs that seemed to take forever. Norah couldn't understand why she felt so impatient, why she seemed to be in such a hurry. It wasn't like her.

After that was finally over, her father took her by the arm as they headed for the limousines, which were lined up outside the church, ready to drive them to the club.

"I heard about Cassidy," he said in a low voice. "How is he?"

"I phoned the hospital this morning," Norah told him. The man had been on her mind most of the night. She hadn't gotten much sleep, which left her with plenty of time to think about Rowdy Cassidy. She'd attributed her restlessness to night-before-the-wedding jitters. She hadn't intended to call the hospital until much later; there was enough to occupy her before the wedding. Valerie had regimented their morning like a drill sergeant, but she'd found a spare moment to make a quick call.

"Carol Franklin was on duty and she told me Rowdy had just come out of surgery."

"And?"

"And he's doing as well as can be expected."

"I thought it might be a good idea if one of us checked up on him later," David Bloomfield said under his breath. "I'll tell Valerie and Colby about the accident myself, after the reception. I'm sure they'll want to see him, too."

"I'll check on him," Norah offered with an eagerness she didn't fully understand.

Her father nodded, and pressed a car key into the palm of her gloved hand. "Steal away when you can. If anyone asks where you are, I'll make up some excuse."

He moved off before Norah could question him. Her father seemed to assume that she'd want to leave the social event of the year, her own sister's wedding, to visit a stranger at the hospital.

And he was right! Without realizing it, she'd been looking for an excuse, a means of doing exactly what her father had suggested. It was the reason she found herself so impatient, so keyed up and restless; she realized that now. Something inside her was calling her back to the hospital. Back to Rowdy Cassidy's bedside.

There was a small break in the wedding festivities between the dinner and the dance. The staff was clearing off the tables and the musicians were tuning up. There should be just enough time for her to leave without anyone's noticing.

Her father caught her eye, and he seemed to be thinking the same thing because he nodded in her direction.

Driving was an exercise in patience with all the layers of taffeta, but Norah managed, although she was sure she made quite a sight.

The hospital was quiet and peaceful when she arrived. If people thought it unusual that she was strolling inside wearing a floor-length rose gown, long white gloves and a broad-brimmed straw hat with a band of ribbon cascading down her back, then they said nothing.

"What room did they put Rowdy Cassidy in?" she asked at the information desk.

"Two fifteen," Janice Wilson told her, after glancing at her computer screen. It was obvious that Janice wanted to ask her a few questions about Valerie and the wedding, but Norah skillfully sidestepped them and hurried down the main hospital corridor.

When she arrived on his floor, she hurried directly into his room. Standing in the darkened doorway, Norah let her eyes adjust to the dim light.

Rowdy's right leg was suspended in the air with a series of levers. His face was turned toward the wall, away from her. Norah walked farther into the room and reached for his medical chart, which was attached to the foot of his bed. She was reading over the notations when she realized intuitively that he was awake. He hadn't made the slightest noise or done anything to indicate he was conscious.

Yet she knew.

Norah moved to the side of his bed, careful not to startle him.

"Hello," she said softly.

His eyes fluttered open.

"Would you like a sip of water?" she asked.

"Please."

She reached for the glass and straw, positioning it at the corner of his mouth. He drank thirstily, and when he finished, raised his eyes to her.

"Am I dead?"

"No," she answered softly, with a reassuring smile. Obviously the medication was continuing to block out the pain, otherwise he'd know exactly how alive he was.

"Should be," he whispered as though speaking demanded a real effort.

"You're a very lucky man, Mr. Cassidy."

He attempted a grin but didn't quite succeed. "Who are you, my fairy godmother?"

"Not quite. I'm Norah Bloomfield, Valerie's sister. And I'm a nurse. I was on call when they brought you in last night."

"Unusual uniform."

Once again Norah found herself smiling. "I was in my sister's wedding this afternoon."

If she hadn't captured his full attention earlier, she did now.

"So Valerie decided to go through with it, after all, did she?"

"Yes."

Silence filled the room.

"Damn fool woman," he muttered after a moment. He turned his head away from her and as he did, Norah noticed that his mouth had tightened with pain. His dark eyes appeared dulled by it.

Norah was left to speculate as to its source, physical or emotional.

CHAPTER TWO

"IN TWENTY YEARS I've never worked with a more disagreeable patient," Karen Johnson was saying when Norah walked into the nurses' lounge early Monday morning. "First off, he refuses the painkiller although the doctor ordered it, then he throws a temper tantrum—and his breakfast tray ends up on the other side of the room!"

"I hope you're talking about a patient in pediatrics," Norah said, sitting down next to her friend.

"Nope. Rowdy Cassidy, the guy they brought in from the plane crash. One thing about him, he's certainly earned his name. By the way, he asked for you. At least I think it was you. He said he wanted to talk to the Bloomfield sister who wore fancy dresses. Since we both know Steffie's more likely to wear jeans, and Valerie's on her honeymoon, he must mean you."

Norah smiled to herself, recalling her brief visit with Rowdy the afternoon of Valerie's wedding. So he remembered.

"Don't feel any obligation to go see him," Karen advised. "In my opinion, the man's been catered to once too often. It'd do him a world of good to acquire a little self-restraint."

From the first, Norah had suspected that Rowdy would be a difficult patient. He was an energetic, decisive man, accustomed to quick action. And he was probably spitting mad about missing Valerie's wedding. He'd been thwarted at every turn, which no doubt added to his deepening frustration.

Although Norah didn't know Valerie's former boss well, she had the distinct impression that he wasn't often foiled. Try as she might, she couldn't help feeling sorry for him. He'd gambled for Valerie's affections and lost. He'd seemed to honestly believe that her sister would have a change of heart and cancel her wedding plans if he came to Orchard Valley.

Norah waited to visit Rowdy until eleven-thirty, when she took her lunch break.

He was lying in bed. His right leg, encased in plaster, was propped at an angle. The blinds were drawn, casting the room into shadow. When he saw her, he levered himself into a sitting position, using a small triangular bar to pull himself upright.

"I heard you wanted to talk to me," she said formally, standing just inside the private room.

He didn't say anything for several moments. "So you were real."

Norah hid a grin and nodded.

"You *are* a nurse, or is this another costume?"

"I'm a nurse."

"Valerie went through with the wedding, didn't she?"

Norah raised her eyebrows. "Of course."

His frown darkened.

"What's this I hear about you throwing the breakfast tray?" she asked, stepping farther into the room.

"Who are you, my mother?" he demanded sarcastically.

"No, but when you behave like a child, you can expect to be treated like one." She walked to the window and twisted open the blinds. Sunlight spilled into the room.

Rowdy shielded his eyes. "The thing with the tray was an accident. Now kindly keep those blinds closed," he barked.

"You're in a black enough mood. My advice to you is to lighten up. Literally."

"I didn't ask for your advice."

"Then I'll give it to you without charge. It wouldn't be a bad idea if you took those pain shots, either. You're not afraid of a needle, are you?"

He scowled fiercely. "Close those blinds, dammit. I need my sleep."

"You aren't going to sleep unless you've got something to help you deal with the pain. Taking a painkiller isn't a sign of weakness, you know. It's common sense."

"I don't believe in drugs."

"I wish we'd known that when you were brought into the emergency room," she said with light sarcasm. "Or when you went into surgery, for that matter. It would have made for an interesting operation, don't you think? What would you've suggested we do? Have you bite into a piece of wood?"

"I'm beginning to detect a bit of family resemblance here," he muttered. "You don't look anything like Valerie, but you're starting to talk just like her."

"I'll accept that as a compliment."

He was clearly growing weaker; levering himself upward must have depleted his strength. Norah was amazed at his ability to move at all.

She neared his bed and rearranged the pillows for him. He slumped back against them and sighed. "Is she happy?"

Norah didn't need Rowdy to explain who he meant by *she*. "I've never seen a more radiant bride," she told him quietly. "They've left for a two-week honeymoon. She and Colby stopped by to check on you before they left, but apparently you were still out of it."

Pain flashed in Rowdy's eyes, and once again Norah was left to wonder if it was from physical discomfort or knowing that he'd truly lost Valerie.

What Rowdy didn't understand, and what Norah couldn't tell him, was that he'd never had a chance with her sister. As far as she was concerned, Valerie's fate had been sealed the minute she met Dr. Colby Winston. Nothing Rowdy said or did from that point forward would have made one iota's difference.

"Where are you going?" Rowdy revived himself enough to demand when she started to leave the room.

"I'll be back," she promised.

True to her word, she returned a couple of minutes later with Karen Johnson following her. Karen's right hand was conspicuously hidden behind her back.

"Get her out of here," he said, snarling at Karen.

"Not just yet," Norah countered smoothly.

Karen hesitated, looking to Norah, who nodded.

"What's that?" he roared when Karen brought her arm forward to reveal the needle. She raised it to the light and squeezed gently until a drop of clear liquid appeared at the tip.

"You, Mr. Cassidy, are about to receive an injection," Norah informed him.

"The hell I am."

Norah thought Rowdy's protest could probably be heard from one end of the hospital to the other, but it didn't deter her or Karen from their task. Norah held Rowdy's arm immobile while Karen swiftly administered the pain medication.

Karen fled the room at the first opportunity. Not so Norah, who dragged a chair to his bedside and sat down. Rowdy was furious and made no attempt to hide his displeasure.

Norah checked her watch and calmly waited. His tirade lasted all of three minutes before he slowed down, slurring his words. His dark eyes glared back at her accusingly.

"Have you finished?" she asked politely, when his voice had dwindled to a mere whisper of outrage.

"Not quite. I'll... both... fired... out of... hospital... for this..."

"I'll give you the name of the hospital administrator, if you like," Norah said helpfully. "It's James Bolton."

He muttered under his breath. She could tell that he was fighting off the effects of the medication. His eyes drifted shut and he snapped them open, scowling at her, only to have his lids close again.

"I want you to know I don't appreciate this," he said, surprising her with a rally of strength.

"I know, but it'll help you sleep and that's what you need."

He was growing more tranquil by the moment. "I thought I'd died," he mumbled.

It *was* a miracle he'd survived the plane crash. Norah was thankful he had, for a number of important reasons.

"You're very much alive, Mr. Cassidy."

"An angel came to see me," he told her, his voice fading. "Dressed in pink. So beautiful...almost made me wish I was dead."

"Sleep now," she urged, her heart constricting at his words. He remembered her visit; he'd mentioned it when she first arrived and now, under the influence of the medication, was talking about it again.

She backed away. Although his eyes were closed, he reached out for her. "Don't go," he mumbled. "Stay...a bit longer. Please."

She gave him her hand and was surprised by the vigor of his grip. Touching him had a curious effect on her. He wasn't in pain now, she knew; the tension had left his face. Norah wasn't sure why she felt compelled to gently brush the hair from his forehead. She was rewarded with a drowsy smile.

"An angel," he mumbled once more. Within seconds he was completely asleep. His grip on her hand relaxed, but it was a long time before Norah left his side.

DAVID BLOOMFIELD, Norah's father, was sitting on the front porch of their large colonial home when she arrived home late that afternoon. He still tired easily from his recent surgery and often sat in the warmth of a summer afternoon, gazing out at his apple orchards.

"How's the patient?" he asked, as Norah climbed the porch steps.

"Physically Mr. Cassidy's improving. Unfortunately I can't say the same thing about his disposition."

David chuckled. "I should give that boy a few
pointers."

Norah grinned. Her father's own stay at the hospital had been a test of his patience—and the staff's.
David hadn't been the most agreeable invalid, especially when he was on the mend. In his eagerness to
return home, he'd often been irritable and demanding. Colby had said wryly that David wanted to make
sure the hospital staff was just as enthusiastic about his
return home as he was himself.

Norah sat on the top step, relaxing for a few minutes. Her day, much of it spent in the emergency
room, had been long and tiring. "Dad," she said
carefully, supporting her back against one of the white
columns, "what did you mean when you told Steffie
that Rowdy Cassidy had arrived right on schedule?"

Her father rocked in his chair for a moment before
answering. "I said that?"

Norah grinned. "According to Steffie you did."

He shrugged. "Then I must have."

She removed her nurse's cap and got to her feet. As
she entered the house, she could hear the sound of her
father's soft chuckle, and wondered what he found so
amusing.

Ever since his open-heart surgery, David Bloomfield had been spouting romantic "predictions" regarding Norah's two older sisters. She hoped he wasn't
intending to do the same with her.

Valerie and Colby had been the first to fit into his
madcap intrigue. Anyone with a nickel's worth of

sense could see what was happening between those two. It didn't take a private detective to see they were falling in love. Naturally there were a few problems, but that was to be expected in any relationship.

When their father awoke from his surgery, however, he claimed he'd visited the afterlife and talked with Grace, the girls' mother, who'd died several years earlier from cancer. He claimed he'd looked into the future and knew exactly whom his three daughters would marry. Colby and Valerie inadvertently lent credibility to his "vision." It made perfect sense to everyone that they'd marry. Certainly no one at the hospital was surprised when Colby gave Valerie Bloomfield an engagement ring. Their father, however, had crowed for a week over the happy announcement.

To complicate matters, a short time later, Steffie and Charles had fallen in love, just as her father had predicted. That case, too, was perfectly logical. Steffie had been in love with Charles for more than three years. Charles had felt the same way toward her.

Norah hadn't been privy to that information, but soon after Steffie arrived home it became apparent she and Charles were meant to be together. It was only logical they'd patch up whatever differences existed between them. Especially since their love had been strong enough to endure a three-year separation.

When Steffie and Charles announced their engagement, David had all but stood up and shouted with glee. Everything was happening just the way he'd said it would, after his near-death experience. Talk about gloating. The man had become impossible ever since. He'd gone so far as to insist that he knew when the grandchildren would begin to arrive. Valerie would be the first, he said; she'd have identical twin sons nine months and three weeks—to the day—after marriage.

He said it was just as well that Rowdy had rejected Valerie as manager of the Pacific Northwest branch, in light of the fact that she was going to be a mother of twins so soon.

No one had known what to say to that, although Valerie had privately assured Steffie and Norah that neither she nor Colby had any intention of starting their family quite so soon.

They'd all decided it was best to let their father think what he wanted. He wasn't hurting anyone, and all his talk about the future seemed to give him pleasure.

Although these proclamations from their father unsettled the Bloomfield sisters, Colby had assured them he'd had other patients who claimed to have experienced near-death encounters. It would all pass in time, he'd said with utter confidence.

Norah couldn't help noticing, however, that her father hadn't said anything to *her* about the man in her life. He'd made some cryptic comment while he was coming out of the anesthesia. He'd smiled up at Norah and mumbled something about six children. Later she realized he was telling her she would someday be the mother of six.

The idea was ludicrous. But he hadn't said a word about it since, which was a relief. She was a medical professional and refused to take his outlandish claims seriously. Neither did she wish to be drawn into discussion concerning them. Besides, anyone who knew the two couples would know they would have married with or without David Bloomfield's dream.

"Rowdy Cassidy's a good man, Norah," her father said from behind her. "Be patient with him."

Pausing, her hand on the screen door, Norah shook her head, trying to force the cowboy, as she still thought of him, from her thoughts. Rowdy was ill-tempered and arrogant, and she wanted as little to do with him as possible. Norah had no intention of becoming personally involved with such a spoiled, ego-centric man. *"Be patient with him."* Norah scoffed silently. If anyone needed to learn a little patience, it was Mr. Rowdy Cassidy.

"THANK GOODNESS you're here," Karen Johnson said to Norah as she barreled through the double doors that led to the emergency room. Her face was red and she was panting slightly, as if she'd run all the way from the second floor.

"What's wrong?"

"It's Mr. Cassidy again. He wants to talk to you as soon as possible."

"That's unfortunate, since I'm on duty."

Karen blinked as if she wasn't sure what she should do next. "I don't think Orchard Valley is ready for a man like Mr. Cassidy."

"What's he done now?"

"He had a phone installed so he could communicate with his company in Texas. Some man arrived late yesterday. I think he's taking up residence.

"Cassidy can barely sit up and already he's conducting business as if he were in some plush office. I'm not exactly sure how it happened, but we all seem to be at his beck and call.''

''What's he want with me?''

''How am I supposed to know?'' Karen snapped. ''It isn't my place to question. My job is to obey.''

Norah couldn't keep from laughing. ''Karen, he's only a man. You've dealt with others just like him a hundred times.''

Karen grumbled and shook her head. ''I've never met anyone like Rowdy Cassidy. Are you coming or not?''

''Not.''

Her friend ran a hand through her disheveled hair. ''I was afraid you were going to say that. Would you reconsider doing it as a personal favor to me?''

''Karen!''

''I'm serious.''

Still Norah hesitated. She wasn't a servant to be summoned by Mr. High-and-Mighty's command. Even if he'd whipped the other members of the hospital staff into shape—the shape of *his* choice—she had no intention of following suit.

''I'll stop in later,'' she said reluctantly.

''How much later?''

''I'll wait until I'm on break.''

Karen's smile revealed her appreciation. ''Thanks, Norah, I owe you one for this.''

Norah wouldn't have believed it if she hadn't seen it herself. A few days earlier, Karen would've given up her retirement to have Rowdy Cassidy removed from her floor. A mere twenty-four hours later, she was running errands for him like an eager cabin boy wanting to keep his pirate captain content.

"You can leave my lunch tray there," Rowdy instructed the candy striper, pointing to his bedside table.

Norah watched the teenager hesitate as though terrified of crossing the threshold into Rowdy's room. Considering what had happened earlier, Norah didn't blame her.

"Come on, now," Rowdy returned impatiently. "I'm not going to bite you."

"I wouldn't believe him, if I were you," Norah said, taking the tray out of the girl's hands.

Rowdy scowled. "It's about time you got here."

"You're lucky I came at all." She didn't like what was happening. Rowdy had manipulated the staff, bullied them into getting his own way, but such methods wouldn't work with her.

"It's been three days. Where have you been?" he demanded, frowning fiercely.

"I didn't know I was obligated to visit you."

"Obligated no, but you must feel a certain moral responsibility."

She set down the tray, and crossed her arms. "I can't say that I do."

He scowled again. "Where was it you said Valerie and her... husband were honeymooning?"

"I didn't."

"Hawaii, I assume? Carlton probably hasn't got an imaginative bone in his body. Which hotel?"

"Carlton?"

"Whoever Valerie married. I'm right, aren't I? They're in Hawaii. Now kindly tell me the name of the hotel."

"You must be joking, Mr. Cassidy. You don't honestly believe I'd be so foolish as to give you the name of the hotel so you could pester my sister on her honeymoon, do you?"

"Aha! So it *is* Hawaii."

Norah winced.

"I just wanted to send a flower arrangement," he went on, his voice a model of sincerity. "And I thought a bottle of champagne would be in order. I'd like to congratulate them, since I missed their wedding."

"A flower arrangement? Champagne? I'll just bet," Norah muttered under her breath.

Rowdy went still for a moment. "You don't know me very well, do you, Ms. Bloomfield? Or you'd appreciate that I'm not the kind of man to begrudge others their happiness. I was a fool to let Valerie go, but now that she's married Carlton, I—"

"Colby," she interrupted.

"Colby," he repeated, dipping his head slightly. "Well, I'd like to offer them both my most heartfelt congratulations."

Norah rolled her eyes. "I don't have the name of their hotel."

Rowdy's gaze hardened briefly. "Then I have no choice but to wait until the happy couple returns from their honeymoon."

"That's an excellent idea." Norah gripped her hands behind her back; she hadn't been completely honest with Rowdy. "Valerie didn't know about your accident until after the wedding," she told him, not quite meeting his eyes.

Rowdy said nothing for several moments. "I didn't think she knew," he said, giving the impression that had she been aware of his injuries, she'd never have gone through with the wedding.

"It wouldn't have made any difference," Norah told him, unable to hide her irritation. "Anyway, she had enough on her mind without having to worry about you, so we decided not to tell her until later."

"You kept it from her?" he stormed.

"That's right, we did," she returned calmly.

He was furious; in fact, Norah had never seen a tantrum to equal his. But she ignored his outburst and went about setting up his luncheon tray. She removed the domed cover from the meal, then folded the napkin and laid it across his chest.

When he paused to breathe, Norah asked, "Do you want your lunch now, or would you prefer to wait until you've calmed down?"

Rowdy's mouth snapped shut.

"Is Dr. Silverman aware you've had a phone brought in for business use? Furthermore, is he aware that you're attempting to work out of this room?"

"No. Are you going to tell him?" he asked, eyeing her skeptically.

"I might."

"It doesn't matter. I'm getting out of this hick town as soon as I can arrange it."

"I'm sure the staff will do everything possible to speed up the process. You've made quite a name for yourself in the past few days, Mr. Cassidy."

Before Rowdy could respond, Karen appeared in the doorway, looking frazzled and uncertain. She glanced at Norah, obviously relieved that her friend was close at hand.

"It's time for your injection, Mr. Cassidy," she said.

"I don't want it."

"I'm sure Mr. Cassidy doesn't mean that, Karen," Norah said cheerfully. "He'll be more than happy to take his shot—isn't that right?"

Rowdy glared at her. "Wrong, Ms. Bloomfield."

"Fine, then. I'll hold him for you, Karen, I only hope I don't bump against his leg, since that would be terribly painful. Of course, if he passes out from the agony, it'll make giving him the injection that much simpler."

"If I take the shot I won't be able to answer the phone," Rowdy growled.

"Might I remind you that you're in the hospital to rest, not to conduct your business affairs?"

Norah took one step toward him, staring at his right leg.

"All right, all right," he grumbled, "but I want you to know I'm doing it under protest. You don't play fair—either one of you."

Karen threw Norah a triumphant look. Rowdy turned his head away while she administered the pain medication. In only minutes the medicine began to take effect.

Rowdy's eyes drifted shut.

"Thanks, Norah," Karen whispered.

"What's going on here?" Norah asked. She'd never known Karen or any of the others to allow a patient to run roughshod over them.

"I wish I knew," Karen muttered. "The only one he's civil to is you. The whole floor's been a madhouse since he arrived. I've never known anyone who can command people the way he does. Even Dr. Silverman seems intimidated."

"Harry?" Norah could hardly believe it.

"I've never looked forward more to a patient's release. The crazy part is that no one's supposed to know he's here. Especially the press. His friend read us the riot act about talking to anyone from the media. They're worried about what'll happen to the stocks."

Norah walked out of Rowdy's room with Karen. Now she understood why the plane crash had received only a brief mention in the news and why Rowdy's name had been omitted. "When will he be able to travel?" she asked.

Karen gave a frustrated shrug. "I don't know, but my guess is it won't be soon. His leg's going to take a long time to heal and the less he moves it now, the better his chances for a complete recovery later. He may end up walking with a cane as it is."

Norah couldn't imagine the proud and mighty Rowdy Cassidy forced to rely on a cane. For his sake, she hoped it wouldn't come to that.

AT HOME that afternoon, Norah was plagued by the thought of a vital man like Rowdy hobbling along with a cane. But she didn't want to think about him. He wasn't her patient and really, other than the fact that her sister had once worked for him, there was no connection between them.

She'd managed to stay away from him for three days, despite the way she felt herself drawn to his presence. She shook her head, bemused. It amazed her that he'd succeeded in causing so much turmoil. The hospital had become a whirlwind of activity and it all seemed to focus on one man. Rowdy Cassidy.

"Hi," Steffie said, breaking into Norah's thoughts.

Norah, who'd been making a salad for their dinner, realized her hands were idle. Her thoughts were on the hospital eleven miles down the road, instead of her task.

"I didn't know if you'd be back for dinner or not," she said, hoping her voice didn't betray the path her mind had taken.

"I wasn't sure, either," Steffie admitted, automatically heading for the silverware drawer. She counted out cutlery and began to set the kitchen table.

Norah continued with the salad, glancing up now and then to watch Steffie. Her sister looked lovelier than ever and her calm, efficient movements revealed a new contentment. A new self-acceptance, really.

So this was what love did. Her sisters seemed to glow with the love they felt—and the love they received. In both of them, natural beauty was enhanced by happiness.

For most of her life, Norah had been referred to as the most attractive of the three Bloomfield girls. She was blond, blue-eyed, petite. But lately, Norah felt plain and downright dowdy compared to Valerie and Stephanie.

"How's everything at the hospital?" Steffie asked absentmindedly.

"I take it you're asking about Rowdy Cassidy?"

Steffie laughed. "I guess I am. You know, I can't help feeling a bit guilty about not giving Valerie his phone message."

"You weren't the only one."

"You didn't give her his message, either? You mean he called more than once? Oh, dear."

"I didn't talk to him," Norah countered swiftly. "But Dad did." Rowdy had never actually said so, but he'd implied that he had phoned Valerie several times. If Steffie had answered one call and Norah none, that left only their dear, meddling father.

She was about to explain that when the phone rang. Norah reached for the receiver; two minutes later she was so furious that she could barely breathe.

Slamming the phone down, she whirled on her sister. "I don't believe this. Of all the high-handed, arrogant—why, it's outrageous."

Steffie frowned. "Norah, what's wrong?"

CHAPTER THREE

"ROWDY CASSIDY has had me transferred out of the emergency room!" Norah shouted, clenching her fists. "The nerve of the man!"

"But why?" Steffie wanted to know.

"So I could be there to wait on him hand and foot like everyone else." Norah stalked angrily to the other side of the kitchen. "I don't believe it! Of all the—"

"Nerve," Steffie supplied.

"Precisely."

"Surely you've got some say in this," Steffie said, as she resumed setting the table. Norah glared at her sister wondering how Steffie could think about dinner at a time like this.

"Apparently I *don't* have a choice in the matter," Norah fumed. "I've been asked to report to Karen Johnson at seven tomorrow morning."

"Oh, dear."

"I'm so furious I could scream."

"What's this yelling all about?" her father asked, strolling into the bright, cheery kitchen.

"It's Rowdy Cassidy again," Steffie explained before Norah had the chance.

David rubbed one hand along his jaw. "I don't think you need to worry—he'll be gone soon enough."

His words were of little comfort to Norah. "Unfortunately, it won't be soon enough to suit me."

Her father chuckled softly and left the kitchen.

NORAH ARRIVED on the second floor early the following morning. Karen Johnson was at the nurses' station making entries on a patient's chart when she caught sight of Norah.

"So you heard."

Norah gave her friend a grumpy smile. "I'm not happy about this."

"I didn't imagine you would be, but what else can we do when His Imperial Highness issues a decree?"

"Is he awake?"

Karen nodded. "Apparently he's been up for hours. He's asked to see you as soon as you got here," Karen said, and made a sweeping motion with her arm.

Although Norah was furious with Rowdy, her friend's courtly gesture produced a laugh. "How's he doing?"

"Better physically. Unfortunately, not so well emotionally. Being stuck in a hick-town hospital, as he so graciously describes Orchard Valley General, hasn't exactly improved his disposition. But then, I think he'd find something to complain about in paradise. He wants out, and there isn't a man or woman on this floor who wouldn't grant him his wish if it was possible."

Norah pushed up the sleeves of her white cardigan sweater as she walked into Rowdy's room, prepared to do battle. He smiled boyishly when he saw her, which disarmed and confused her. She hadn't expected him to be in a good mood.

"Morning," he greeted her brightly.

"I want you to know I don't appreciate the fact that you've adjusted my life to suit your own purposes."

"What?" he demanded. "Asking the administrator to assign you to this floor? You were the one who gave me his name, weren't you? Aren't you being a bit selfish?"

"Me? If *I'm* selfish, what does that make you?"

"Lonely. You're the only person I know in this entire town."

"Your acquaintance is with my sister, not me," she forcefully reminded him.

"In this case, it's any port in the storm. I trust you, Norah, though, Lord help me, I'm not sure why. You've already admitted Valerie didn't know about my accident because you didn't tell her until after the wedding. I can only assume you wanted me for yourself."

If he was hoping she'd rise to his bait, he had a long wait coming. She folded her arms and expelled a deep sigh. "I'll be bringing your breakfast in a couple of minutes," she said, turning her back on him.

When she returned a few minutes later, carrying the tray, Rowdy was sitting up in bed. "I need your help," he announced.

"You look perfectly capable of feeding yourself."

"I'm bored out of my mind."

"Do what everyone else does, watch television," she said tartly. Whether he was lonely or not, she refused to pander to his moods. He'd pulled a dirty trick on her and she wasn't going to reward his behavior.

Rowdy glanced up at the blank television screen. "Please don't be annoyed with me, Norah. I'm serious."

"So am I." But she could feel herself weakening. Rowdy could turn on the charm, and when he did, Norah suspected, few would deny him. Karen Johnson, for instance... Norah had no intention of ending up the same way.

"When will you be back?" he asked, grimacing as he examined his meal. The toast was cold. Norah could tell by the way the butter sat hard and flat on top. The eggs were runny and the oatmeal looked like paste. Norah didn't envy him.

"Someone else will be by to pick up your tray in a little while," she answered him.

"You might as well take it now."

"Try and eat something," she suggested sympathetically.

"What? The half-cooked eggs or the lumpy oatmeal? No thanks, I'd rather go without."

"Lunch will be more appetizing," Norah promised.

His brows arched cynically. "Wanna bet?"

Norah left his room, but she came back a few minutes later with two homemade blueberry muffins. Rowdy's eyes lit up when she set them on his breakfast tray. "I can't believe I'm doing this," she muttered.

"Where'd you get those?" As if he feared she'd change her mind, he snatched one off the tray.

"I baked last night and brought them in for the staff for coffee break this morning. Enjoy."

"I intend to." Already he was peeling away the paper. The first muffin disappeared in three bites. "These are wonderful," he said, licking the crumbs from his fingers. "Ever thought about selling the recipe?"

Norah laughed. The recipe had been her mother's and Norah strongly suspected it had originally come from a magazine. "Not lately."

"Well, if you ever do, let me know." He was ready to dig into the second offering. "By the way, Kincade's stopping by this afternoon, so hold off on those damn pain shots, will you?"

"Kincade?"

"My corporate attorney. Being stuck here is frustrating as hell. Kincade and I spoke yesterday and he's hand-carrying some papers that have to be signed, so I'm going to need a clear head. Got that?"

"Yes, Your Highness."

Rowdy frowned, but said nothing.

His phone rang, the sound muted. Norah watched, amazed, as Rowdy ignored the hospital phone on his bedstand and pulled open the drawer, from which he removed a portable telephone. After a few preliminary greetings, he was lost in conversation, unaware she was still in the room.

Norah shrugged, then gathered up the tray and left.

The morning passed quickly and she didn't talk to Rowdy again until near the end of her shift, at three. He was tired and out of sorts. His attorney friend had spent two hours with him, and an exhausted Rowdy had slept fitfully afterward.

"He's much calmer when you're around," Karen commented as they prepared to leave.

Norah didn't believe for a moment that she'd made the slightest difference to Rowdy's behavior. If Karen wanted to thank anyone, it should be Kincade, who'd kept him occupied; at least when he was busy he didn't have time to make everyone else miserable.

On impulse she decided to check on him before she left for home. He was sitting up, listlessly flipping through channels on the television. Apparently nothing appealed to him.

"I didn't know daytime television was in such desperate straits," he muttered when he saw her. He pushed another button and the screen went blank. "I was hoping you'd stop by before you went home."

"How are you feeling?" she asked, trying to gauge his mood. He seemed somewhat revived from the nap.

"Lousy."

Norah was surprised he'd admit it. "Do you want a pain shot?"

He shook his head. "But I wouldn't mind a little distraction. Can you sit down and talk for a few minutes?"

Norah made a show of glancing at her watch, although in reality she hadn't a single reason to hurry home. "I can stay a little while, I guess." She certainly wasn't being gracious about it, but that didn't seem to bother Rowdy.

"Good."

Norah was met with the full force of his smile, and for a moment she basked in its warmth. It was little wonder he inspired such loyalty and confidence in his employees. He definitely had the charisma of true leadership. Valerie had worked with him for nearly four years, dedicating her time and talent to his corporation until she virtually had no life of her own. She'd done it voluntarily, too, inspired by Rowdy's own commitment to CHIPS.

"How'd the meeting with your friend go?" Norah asked conversationally.

He paused as though he'd never considered Kincade his friend. "Fine. Actually, it went very well. We've been able to keep the news of my accident from leaking to the press."

"What would be so terrible about anyone finding out you're in the hospital?" Norah shrugged. "Karen mentioned something about the stocks."

Rowdy cast her an odd look as though he suspected she was teasing. "You honestly don't know?" He shook his head. "If the stockholders discovered I was incapacitated, they'd lose confidence in CHIPS and the stock could drop by several points."

"Would that really be so disastrous?"

"Yes," he returned without hesitation. "If the value declines by even a single point, that's equivalent to losing millions of dollars. Any greater loss and it becomes catastrophic, with a ripple effect that could rock the entire industry."

Either the man had an elevated sense of his own worth, or he was pessimistic by nature. Though perhaps she was being unnecessarily harsh, Norah mused. She knew next to nothing about business and finance. Nor did she care. She was content to leave the world's financial affairs in the capable hands of people like Rowdy Cassidy and her sister. She stood abruptly and walked toward the door.

"Do you have to go so soon?" Rowdy asked, disappointment in his dark eyes.

"I'll be right back," she promised.

It took her several minutes to find what she was looking for.

Rowdy brightened when she returned. "What's that?" he asked, nodding toward the rather battered box she was carrying.

"You do play games, don't you?"

"Often, but I seldom need a board."

Norah laughed lightly. "Then I promise you this is right up your alley. It's a game of power, intrigue and skill." She set the box on the foot of his bed and slowly, dramatically, lifted the lid. She had Rowdy's full attention now.

"Checkers?" he asked with more than a hint of disbelief.

"Checkers." She drew the bedside table closer, moved some flowers and placed the board on it. Then she pulled up a chair. "You want red or black?"

"Black to match my evil temperament." Rowdy gave an exaggerated leer, twirling an imaginary mustache.

Norah grinned. "I'm not going to argue with you."

They set up the board together. "Generally when I play a game there's something riding on the outcome," he said in a relaxed, offhand manner.

"Like what?" Norah pushed a red checker one space forward.

"Usually the stakes are big. It makes the game more...interesting."

"Are you suggesting we wager something on the outcome of this game?" She'd forgotten how competitive men could be.

"Something small—this time," he said, studying the board.

"Give me an example." It'd been a while since she'd played checkers and she wasn't all that sure of her skills. She'd never taken games, any game, too seriously.

"I don't know..." Rowdy paused, apparently mulling it over. "How about dinner?"

"Dinner? You mean after you're discharged from the hospital?"

"No, I mean tonight."

Norah snickered. "What are you planning to do? Order up a second tray from the kitchen? If that's the case, I'm afraid I'll have to decline the invitation."

"I won't need to order you another dinner tray," he stated calmly, making his first jump and capturing one of her checkers. "I intend to win."

Rowdy did exactly that, and his winning streak continued, even when they decided the wager was two games out of three. After her second loss, Rowdy leaned back against the pillows, folded his arms and threw her a self-satisfied smile. "I'd like rare roast beef, a baked potato with sour cream, green beans, fresh if possible, and three-layer chocolate cake for dessert, preferably with coconut frosting. Homemade would be nice. Do you have a recipe for good chocolate cake?"

Stepping away from his bed, Norah settled her fists on her hips. "Is this your usual diet? Good grief, you're a prime candidate for a heart attack. I'll bet you don't exercise, either."

"Not recently." He looked pointedly at his leg. "Are you going to honor your end of the bargain or not?"

"I'm not sure yet. I'll bring your dinner, but don't hold your breath waiting for rare roast beef."

"I'm a Texan," he challenged. "I was weaned on prime rib."

"Then it's high time you started checking your cholesterol, cowboy. My father recently went through open-heart surgery and it wasn't any picnic. My advice to you is to make a change in your eating habits now."

"All right, all right," Rowdy grumbled. "I'll settle for pizza and to show you just how reasonable I can be, go ahead and order it with those little fish. That's healthy, right?"

"Anchovies? Do you realize how high in sodium anchovies are?"

"There's no satisfying you, is there?" Rowdy chuckled. "If it isn't my cholesterol level you're fussing about, it's sodium count or something. Before you leave, you'll have me on a diet of bread and water, which is basically the only food I've been eating since I got in here, anyway."

Norah found herself laughing again. "I'll see to my dad's dinner and be back later with your pizza," she promised on her way out the door.

"Bring that checkerboard," he told her. "There're a few other wagers I'd like to make."

Norah had a few of her own. If everything went according to her plans, Rowdy would be as docile as a sleepy cat before he left Orchard Valley Hospital.

"You're later than usual," her father commented when Norah walked into the house. "Problems at the hospital?"

"Not really." She wasn't sure how much she should say to him about her time with Rowdy. Her own confusion didn't help. The man was in love with her sister, for heaven's sake! And he annoyed her no end with his tactics. It didn't make sense that she should find herself attracted to him.

"I have to go back to the hospital," she explained on her way upstairs, deciding not to offer any further explanation. She wanted a long bath, a short nap and a change of clothes, in that order.

"Don't worry about dinner," David called up after her. "I can take care of it. Plenty of leftovers in the refrigerator. Besides, I had a big lunch, so I don't have too much of an appetite."

Norah hesitated at the top of the stairs. Her father was right; he was now fully capable of looking after himself. The last thing he needed was her fussing over him. It came as something of a shock to realize that. Then she smiled. It came as a relief, too.

THE HOSPITAL was quiet when Norah returned a couple of hours later. The head floor nurse smiled when she saw her carrying a boxed pizza. "I wondered what you promised him," LaVern joked. "He's been as good as gold all evening."

Opening the door with a flourish, Norah marched into Rowdy's room, balancing the pizza on the palm of one hand. "Ta da!"

Rowdy reached for the triangular bar dangling above his head and pulled himself upright. "I was beginning to think you were going to renege on our bet."

"A Bloomfield? Never!" She set the pizza box on the table and wheeled it to his side. "However I must warn you this pizza is healthy for you."

"Oh, great, you've ordered granola and broccoli for the toppings."

"Close. Mushroom, green pepper, onion. I had them put anchovies on your half. Personally I think you should appreciate my thoughtfulness. I can't stand those slimy little fish things—they're disgusting."

"Don't worry. I won't force you to eat any."

"Good."

Rowdy helped himself to a napkin and lifted the first slice from the box. He raised it slowly to his mouth, then closed his eyes, as if in ecstasy, as he chewed. "This is excellent, just excellent."

"I demand a rematch," Norah said, dragging her chair to his bedside. "When we're finished eating. Winning is a matter of personal pride now."

"Sore loser," he muttered through a mouthful of pizza.

"What!" Norah felt the annoyance bubble up inside her. Apparently Rowdy noticed it, too, because he grinned at her. "I was teasing," he assured her. "Believe me, the last thing I want to do now is bite the hand that feeds me."

"You ready for another challenge, then?" Norah asked, eager to clear away the remains of the pizza and set up the board.

"Any time you want, sweetheart."

Norah didn't think he meant the term as one of affection and decided to ignore it. At least that was her intention . . .

But more than once she found her concentration drifting away from the game. Before she could stop herself, she wondered what it would be like to be Rowdy Cassidy's "sweetheart." He was opinionated and headstrong, but he could charm the birds out of the trees, as her mother used to say. He was also a man who almost always got what he wanted—Valerie Bloomfield being one of the few exceptions. Norah felt oddly deflated, suddenly, as she recalled his feelings for her sister.

Almost before she realized it, she'd lost two games in a row. Not until she made a silly mistake that cost her the second game did she realize they hadn't set their wager.

"What are you going to want next?" she muttered, irritated with herself for losing so easily. "I could bring you in another blueberry muffin tomorrow morning."

Rowdy's smile was downright smug.

"How about three games out of five?" she asked hopefully.

"A deal's a deal."

"Now that's profound," Norah said in a sarcastic aside. "All right." She spread both hands in a gesture of defeat. "You won. I'm not sure how fair or square it was, but you won."

"My, my, are you getting testy?"

She couldn't very well admit why she'd been so distracted. She stared down at the board as she rapidly gathered up the checkers. When she'd finished, he reached for her hands, capturing them between his own, drawing her closer to his side. She knew she should protest, or make some effort to pull away from him. But she found it difficult to move, to speak, to do anything but gaze into his eyes.

"I'm going to kiss you, Norah Bloomfield," he announced in a quiet, dispassionate voice. "I want that even more than I wanted the pizza." He gave her hands a tug and she found herself sitting on the edge of the bed. Her heart was pounding hard against her ribs, her breath coming in short, painful bursts.

His mouth settled over hers, his hands in her hair, pressing her close against him. Norah was shocked by the powerful sensuality she experienced. Her eyes closed slowly as excitement overtook common sense.

She didn't doubt for an instant that if she'd given the least protest Rowdy would have released her. His mouth was warm, hard, compelling...

When the kiss ended, she automatically rose to her feet and backed away. She blinked, feeling oddly confused. "Th-that was...unfair," she stammered.

"Unfair? In what way?" he demanded.

"You didn't set the terms of the wager—I wasn't prepared for it!"

"You needed a warning?"

She pressed the tips of her fingers to her lips, at a loss to explain herself. "I'm...not sure. Yes, I think so." She still felt dazed and it made her furious.

"Norah, what's wrong?"

"I don't think playing checkers was such a good idea, after all," she said coldly, recovering as well as she could. Her hands trembled as she hurriedly finished putting away the game. It wasn't until she felt a tear roll down the side of her face that she realized she was crying, and that only served to mortify her further.

"I didn't mean to offend you," Rowdy said, his voice regretful.

"Then why'd you do it? Why couldn't we just be friends? Why does everything have to boil down to... to that?"

"You're making more of this than necessary," he said softly. "I'm sorry if I upset you. That was never my intention, and it won't happen again."

Suddenly Norah wasn't sure she wanted that reassurance. She wasn't sure *what* she wanted; that was the problem. As much as she hated to admit it, she'd enjoyed the kiss.

"We heard from Valerie and Colby," she said abruptly.

He frowned. "Are they having a good time?"

She didn't meet his eyes. "Perfectly wonderful."

"Valerie's going to be bored out of her mind within a month, you know that, don't you?"

Norah shook her head.

"I told her as much when she handed me her resignation." His frown deepened. "She knows it, too."

"Valerie will find something else."

"In Orchard Valley? Don't count on it. Not with her qualifications. What's she going to do? Run the school lunch program?" Rowdy was growing more animated by the minute. "Damn fool woman, letting her emotions dictate her life. I expected better of her."

"My sister made her choice, Mr. Cassidy. If anyone was a fool, it's you."

His mouth tightened at her words and Norah marveled that they could be wrapped in each other's arms one moment and snapping at each other the next.

"She and this Carlton fellow will be very happy, I'm sure," Rowdy said stiffly. He leaned back against the pillows and grimaced in obvious pain.

"It's Colby."

"Whoever," he muttered irritably.

Norah realized it was the discomfort speaking now, and relaxed. "I'll ask LaVern to bring you something for the pain."

"I don't need anything," he growled.

"Perhaps not, but as a favor to me, please take it."

"I don't owe you anything."

Norah was offended at the sharpness of his tone. He glared at her as if he couldn't wait to be rid of her, reminding her once again that it was her sister he was interested in—not her.

"All right," he said curtly. "I'll take the damn shot. Just stop looking at me like I've done something terrible. It was only a kiss! Good Lord, you'd think no one had ever kissed you before."

At his words, Norah understood. That was exactly the way she felt, as if Rowdy Cassidy had been the first man to hold her. The first man to kiss her. It was as if she'd waited all her life for this moment, this man.

Before she could stop herself, she turned and rushed from the room.

NORAH DREADED the following morning, since she was again scheduled to report to Rowdy's floor. She avoided seeing him as long as possible—an entire fifteen minutes into her shift.

"Good morning," she greeted him with a bright smile.

"Sounds like you're in better spirits than you were the last time I saw you," he said, watching her closely.

"Having one's ego destroyed in a game of checkers will do that," Norah said with false cheerfulness, carrying his breakfast tray to the bedside table.

"Was it the checkers . . . or the kiss?"

"It looks like lumpy oatmeal and soft-boiled eggs this morning," she said, ignoring his words.

"Norah." His hand covered hers, preventing her from leaving.

"The checkers," she said dryly. "You flatter yourself if you think a kiss would unsettle me like that. I'm a big girl, Mr. Cassidy."

"Then perhaps we should try again."

"Don't be absurd."

Rowdy's hand tightened over hers. "It isn't as preposterous as you make it sound. You're very sweet, Norah Bloomfield. A man could grow accustomed to having you around."

Norah hesitated, not knowing if she should take his words as a compliment or an insult. "I'm not a plaything for your personal amusement. Now if you'll excuse me, I've got work to do."

"Will you stop by later?"

"If I have the time." Her back was to him; she was eager to make her escape.

"If you bring the checkers game I'll give you another chance to redeem yourself. I might even let you win just so I can give you what *you* want."

"Ah, but that's where we differ," she said as breezily as she could. "You see, Mr. Cassidy, you don't have anything I want."

"Ouch," he said and as she left the room she glanced over her shoulder to see him clutching at an imaginary wound. She didn't want to laugh, but she couldn't help herself.

Three hours had passed when Karen Johnson sought her out. "Check on the cowboy, would you, Norah? Something's wrong."

"Why me?" Norah protested.

"You're the only one who can go near him without getting your head ripped off."

"Did he ask for me?"

Karen hesitated. "Yes, but don't feel complimented. He's throwing out plenty of names, including the governor's and a couple of congressmen. It wouldn't surprise me if they rushed to his side, either."

Karen hadn't exaggerated. By the time Norah arrived from the far end of the corridor, she could hear Rowdy ranting about something. His words, however, were indistinguishable, which in Norah's opinion was probably for the best.

"Rowdy," she said, standing in the doorway, her hands on her hips. "What's going on in here?"

He glanced up at her, placing his hand on the portable telephone's mouthpiece. "Word leaked out that I was in a plane crash." He sighed heavily. "CHIPS stock has already dropped two points. We're in one hell of a mess here."

CHAPTER FOUR

"Do you know of a decent secretarial service?" Rowdy demanded as soon as Norah walked in the door the following morning. He might have been sitting behind a mahogany desk preparing to command his empire. His dark eyes were sharp and alert, his jaw tense.

"Uh . . . I don't think so."

"What I need is a phone book."

Taken aback, Norah twisted around and pointed behind her. "There's one at the end of the hall."

"Get it," he said, then added. "Please."

Still Norah hesitated. "Rowdy, you seem to have forgotten you're in the hospital and not a hotel."

"I wouldn't care if I was in the morgue. I'm not about to watch the business I built up—ten years of blood and sweat—go down the tube because of a stupid broken leg."

"Your leg's far more than—"

"The telephone book," he reminded her crisply.

Norah tossed her hands in the air and retrieved the phone book from the nurses' station.

"This is it?" Rowdy's eyes widened incredulously when she handed it to him. "I've read short stories longer than this."

"There's always Portland, but to be honest I don't know where I'd find a Portland directory."

"Kincade and Robbins are flying in. They'll be here by noon. I hate to ask Mrs. Emerich to travel, but I may not have any choice. Advise the hospital that I'll be holding a press conference this afternoon." He rubbed the side of his jaw, his look thoughtful. "While you're at it, would you arrange to have a barber drop by sometime this morning? I'm going to need a decent haircut and a shave."

"Rowdy, this is a hospital."

"Not anymore," he told her flatly.

"I don't have time to be running errands for you. In case you've forgotten, you're not the only patient on this floor. I can't allow you to disrupt the entire wing with camera crews and the like."

"The excitement will do them good," he told her, leafing through the Orchard Valley directory. "It'll give your patients something to tell their families during visiting hours."

Norah was beginning to get irritated. "You're not listening to me."

He went on as if she hadn't spoken, his eyes narrowed and resolute. "I'm going to hold a press conference and if I can't do it from here, I'll find someplace I can."

"You can't be moved."

"Don't bet on it, sweetheart."

Norah didn't, not for an instant. Rowdy would have his way, simply because he made it impossible to oppose him and win.

Norah left him and reported what he'd told her to Karen Johnson. Afterward, she was never entirely sure what happened next. But before the morning ended, the hospital administrator, James Bolton, had visited Rowdy's room. Norah had no way of knowing what was discussed, but she learned a little later that a number of reporters and two camera crews would be brought into Rowdy's room early that same afternoon. Just as he'd predicted.

Orchard Valley General Hospital had never seen anything like it. Charles Tomaselli, Steffie's fiancé, showed up, and cornered Norah to ask if she could get him into the press conference.

Norah shrugged. "I'll try." She did and was rewarded with a thumbs-up sign from Charles.

By two that afternoon, the entire ward looked more like a media carnival than a hospital.

"Did you ever dream it'd come to this?" Karen asked her, leaning against the counter at the nurses' station as she viewed the proceedings.

Norah shook her head. She didn't know if Rowdy had the physical stamina to withstand a lengthy interview. The news conference had been going on for nearly an hour, with no sign of ending anytime soon.

Reporters were crammed inside his hospital room, spilling out into the hallway, and jostling one another, cassette recorders held high above their heads. Cameras flashed.

The patients from the other rooms stood in their doorways, gawking, trying to find out what they could. Rumors washed like flash floods through the hospital corridors.

At one point Norah heard the president was visiting. Someone else claimed royalty had arrived. Two other people were convinced they'd seen Elvis.

From the corner of her eye, Norah saw Kincade, Rowdy's corporate attorney. He seemed to be searching through the crowd, looking for someone. Intuitively, she realized what was happening. Rowdy had worn himself out.

"Excuse me," Norah said, thinking and acting quickly. Carrying a tray in one hand and a syringe in the other, she edged her way through the reporters and camera crews. The news staff reluctantly parted to make a path for her. She moved into the room, then held up one hand to shade her eyes from the blinding light. It didn't take her an instant to realize Kincade's concerns were well founded. Rowdy was pale and definitely growing weaker, although he struggled to disguise it.

"You'll have to excuse me," she said in her most businesslike voice. "I'm sure this will only take a couple of minutes. It's time for Mr. Cassidy's enema."

The room cleared within seconds.

Rowdy waited until the last reporter had left, then burst out laughing. Kincade and the other man Rowdy had referred to as Robbins were the only two who remained.

"Very clever," Kincade complimented her.

"She isn't worth a damn at checkers, but she's one hell of a nurse," Rowdy said. He lowered himself onto the pillows and closed his eyes in exhaustion. "You'll arrange everything for me, Robbins?" he asked hoarsely.

"Right away," the other man assured him.

Briefly, Nora wondered if Rowdy even knew the first names of his staff members. It was Kincade and

Robbins. But then, he'd always referred to his sister as Valerie. He knew *her* first name.

She was about to comment, but she noticed Rowdy was already asleep. Without another word, she ushered the two men out of the room.

"Thanks," Kincade whispered gratefully.

She nodded. It was her job to look out for the welfare of her patients. She hadn't done anything extraordinary. Her means might have been a little unorthodox, but effective.

Robbins was tall and wiry and young, and Kincade was short, stocky and middle-aged. Both men were dressed in identical dark, pin-striped suits—the CHIPS uniforms, Norah thought wryly. She remembered her sister's wearing the female version of that business suit. Though, strangely, Norah couldn't imagine Rowdy in anything but jeans and cowboy boots.

"I understand you're Valerie's sister," Robbins said in a conversational tone.

"That's right." She'd forgotten that the two men had probably worked with Valerie.

"We all miss her."

But not as much as Rowdy does, Norah mused and was surprised by a sharp, fleeting pain at the thought.

"Rowdy's transferring me to Portland to head up the expansion project," Robbins said, eyeing Norah as if she had information to give. "I was hoping that once I got settled, Valerie would consider working with me."

"I don't know," Norah told him. "You'll have to talk to my sister."

Robbins glanced nervously toward Rowdy's room. "Don't say anything to Rowdy. Valerie was by far the more logical choice, but I don't think those two parted on amicable terms. He accepted her resignation and then gave me the assignment that same day. Personally, I'd rather stay in Texas."

It went without saying that Robbins would move simply because Rowdy had asked it of him. Oregon. Alaska. Wherever. Whatever other talents Rowdy possessed, and Norah didn't doubt there were many, he inspired loyalty among his employees.

"Valerie and her husband are on their honeymoon. She should be back from Hawaii sometime this week. You might have the opportunity to tell her all this yourself," Norah said, then turned away.

"Ms.—Bloomfield."

This time it was the corporate attorney who addressed her. "Thanks again," he said.

"No problem. I was happy to be of help."

"This isn't easy for him, you know?" the attorney added. "Rowdy's a physical man and being tied down to his bed, literally, is driving him to distraction. If it wasn't for you, I don't know what he would have done."

"Wasn't for me?" Norah hadn't done much of anything. She'd provided a little entertainment with the checkers, a little nourishment with the pizza and muffins, and she'd fallen into his schemes, like everyone else in the hospital. But that was it.

"He's mentioned you several times. All of us at CHIPS want you to know we appreciate everything you've done for him."

Norah nodded, accepting his gratitude, but she felt uncomfortably like a fraud. Rowdy must have greatly exaggerated the small things she'd done.

LATER THAT AFTERNOON, just before she was scheduled to be relieved from her shift, the office equipment began to arrive. First came a fax machine, followed by a computer, complete with printer. Then two men carrying a desk with an inverted chair balanced on top passed her in the corridor.

"What's going on *now?*" Karen asked, rubbing her eyes as if she were seeing things.

"I have the feeling," Norah muttered, "that Rowdy Cassidy is about to set up office."

Norah followed the desk and chair to Rowdy's room and stood staring in amazement at the transformation. He'd done exactly what she'd suspected. This wasn't a hospital room any longer, but a communications center. A man from the telephone company was busy installing a multiline phone. Heaven only knew how many extra lines Rowdy had ordered. Apparently he'd outgrown the portable phone he kept in his drawer.

"I hate to intrude," she muttered sarcastically, "knowing how busy you are and all—but *what* is going on in here?"

"What does it look like?" Rowdy returned curtly. "I'm getting back to work."

"Here?"

"I don't have much choice. Robbins will be in bright and early tomorrow with my secretary. I'll be handling as many of my own affairs as I can."

"I only hope Dr. Silverman and the rest of the hospital staff don't get in your way."

Rowdy didn't hear the sarcasm in her voice, or if he did, he ignored it. Norah sighed.

"Rowdy, this is a hospital. You're here to recover so you can go back to your life. You can't go around conducting business as usual. I'm sorry, I really am, but—"

"Either I conduct my business or there won't be one to go back to," he announced starkly.

"You're exaggerating."

"All four lines are connected and working," the telephone installer said, setting the phone on the bedside table and rolling it within reaching distance.

"Thank you," Rowdy said as the man walked out the door. "Listen, Norah, you're a damn good nurse," he continued, "but you don't know... checkers about managing a corporation. Now loosen up, before I let everyone know what a poor sport you are."

Norah felt the warmth invade her cheeks.

"This all right over here?" one of the men who'd hauled in the desk interrupted.

"Perfect," Rowdy answered, barely glancing in that direction. "Thank you for your trouble."

"No problem." The two men left, closing the door behind them. As soon as he was alone with her, Rowdy reached for Norah's hand. "Have you recovered?" he asked, his eyes holding hers.

"I'm not the one who's sick."

"I meant from the kiss."

His comment intensified the heat in her face. "I—I don't know what you're talking about."

"Yes, you do. You've been thinking about it every minute since." He added in a whisper, "So have I."

"Uh..." What bothered Norah most was how accurate he was. She'd spent a lot of time reflecting on their kiss, despite all her efforts to push it from her mind. She'd dreaded being alone with Rowdy again, fearing he'd know how confused and flustered his touch had left her.

"You're a beautiful woman, Norah." He pressed her palm to his lips. The feel of his tongue against her skin sent hot sensation shooting up her arm.

Norah trembled and closed her eyes. He was drawing her closer to his side and like an obedient lamb she went to him. He reached for her and from somewhere deep inside, she found the strength to resist.

"No...no, Rowdy. I'm Norah, not Valerie. I don't think you've figured out the difference yet." Hurriedly she backed away from him and left the room. He called for her once, his voice sharp with impatience, but Norah ignored him.

THE AFTERNOON was overcast and gloomy; rain threatened. Norah found her father sitting in his favorite chair beside the fireplace in his den, reading.

"I understand there was quite a commotion at the hospital this afternoon," he said, glancing up from Marcia Muller's latest mystery.

"You heard? Already?"

"Charles stopped in and gave Steffie and me a rundown of what happened. Sounds like a three-ring circus."

"It was ridiculous."

Her father chuckled. "I also heard how you broke up the news conference. I always knew you were a clever child, I just don't think I fully appreciated *how* clever."

"Rowdy Cassidy's impossible."

"Oh?" Although the question appeared casual, Norah wasn't fooled. Her father was doing his best to gauge how the relationship was developing between her and Rowdy. The situation with Rowdy was very like his own thirty years earlier, when he'd met Grace, who'd been a nurse, and married her. Theirs had been a hospital romance. Although her father hadn't said much, Norah knew he was hoping history would repeat itself.

In a way it troubled Norah that he hadn't questioned her more about her relationship with Valerie's former employer. She should have been relieved. He'd barely asked about Rowdy, barely revealed any interest. Nor had he mentioned his near-death dream lately, other than that one cryptic remark about Rowdy's arriving right on schedule. She certainly didn't believe her father's dream—in which he'd supposedly had a conversation, complete with predictions about all three sisters. But it had sustained him and delighted him for so long that she actually found his silence disturbing.

Norah drifted up the stairs to her room. She wished now that she'd allowed Rowdy to kiss her. And yet it angered her that she should be feeling anything—especially when she knew how deeply Rowdy cared for Valerie.

Norah changed out of her uniform and walked slowly down the back stairs that led to the spacious kitchen. Halfway down, she heard Steffie and Charles. They were speaking in low tones, and their words were followed by silences. Lovers exchanging promises.

Not wanting to embarrass them, or herself, Norah made sure they heard her approach. She burst onto the scene with a bright smile to find her sister sitting in Charles's lap. A wooden spoon coated in spaghetti sauce was poised in front of his mouth.

With obvious reluctance, Charles dragged his gaze away from Steffie. "Thanks for getting me into that press conference this afternoon, Norah. I appreciate it."

"No problem." She opened the refrigerator and took out a pitcher of lemonade. Her back to the happy couple, she heard Steffie whisper something, then giggle softly.

"What time's dinner?" Norah asked, refusing to look in their direction. She got a tall glass and added ice before pouring the lemonade.

"Another hour or so."

She couldn't face Steffie and Charles just now. Seeing how happy they were, how much in love, was almost painful. "Do you need any help with dinner?"

"No, thanks," Charles answered for Steffie. "We've got everything under control here."

Norah was sure they had.

It wasn't until she was in her bedroom with the door closed that she realized how tense and rigidly controlled she'd been.

Steffie and Charles's wedding was only a few weeks away, and she was excited and happy for them both. They hadn't wanted the elaborate affair Valerie and

Colby had had. It was just as well, since Orchard Valley had yet to recover from the first Bloomfield wedding.

Norah was happy for her sisters. Really happy. They both deserved the love they'd found.

Love.

It had changed Valerie, turned her entire life upside down. Her oldest sister had never been one to reveal her emotions, but from the moment Valerie had accepted Colby's engagement ring, she'd changed. She'd become exuberant, animated. Right before Norah's eyes, love had transformed her sister into someone she barely recognized. Valerie, who'd always been so serious, so business minded, had become giddy with love.

It had the opposite effect on Steffie. Her middle sister had always been the emotional one. No one doubted what Steffie was thinking. She'd never had any qualms about expressing her opinions.

These days Steffie was calm and peaceful. When she was with Charles, she seemed to be a different woman, Norah thought. Her sister had always been in a hurry; there were people to meet, places to go, experiences to live. But no longer. She'd relaxed, slowed down.

Both her sisters were marrying men who balanced them. Men whose personalities complemented and completed theirs.

And then there was Norah.

Expelling her breath, Norah stretched out on her bed and stared at the ceiling. She dated often, but none of the men she was currently seeing affected her the way Colby and Charles had affected her sisters. Still, after watching what had happened to them, she wasn't sure what to expect in her own life. Should she expect her personality to be moderated, too? And in what way? She'd never been as serious as Valerie, or as vivacious as Steffie. She was just plain Norah.

The phone rang, but the first ring was abruptly cut off. A moment later, Steffie came pounding up the stairs, yelling, "Norah! Phone!"

Norah rolled over and reached for the phone on her bedside table. "Hello," she mumbled.

"Do you feel up to a game of checkers?"

"Rowdy?" Her heart quickened at the sound of his voice.

He chuckled. "You mean you've been playing games with other men? I'm shocked."

"I..." She didn't know what to say. Instinct told her to say yes, to agree to another game immediately. But common sense intervened. "No," she told him firmly.

"I promise no more tricks," he said as a means of inducement.

"I'm sorry. I don't think so."

There was a long silence before he spoke again. "I had another reason for calling. I wanted to thank you for everything you did this afternoon."

"It wasn't that much."

"But it helped, and I'm grateful. I've caused quite a ruckus in the orderly world of this hospital, haven't I?"

"Indeed you have," she said with a soft laugh. She had a sneaking suspicion it was the same wherever he went—Orchard Valley, Houston, Texas or New York City.

Rowdy chuckled, too, and then asked her a couple of questions, about the hospital and the town; she answered and asked him a few of her own. The conversation continued in a casual vein.

After what seemed like only minutes, Norah heard Steffie calling her down for dinner. Norah glanced at her watch, amazed to discover she'd been talking to Rowdy for nearly half an hour.

"I have to go."

"Well, thanks again . . . Norah." He said her name with an odd, breathless catch. "I always seem to be thanking you."

Running down the stairs toward the kitchen, Norah realized she felt completely revived.

It felt as though everyone—her father, Charles and Steffie—turned to stare at her when she walked into the room. "Is something wrong?" she asked, glancing down to be sure her blouse wasn't incorrectly buttoned.

"Not a thing," her father said, reaching for the green salad. "Nope, not a thing." But Norah saw him raise his eyes to Steffie and grin from ear to ear.

ROWDY'S ROOM had been transformed into a command post. Men and women were walking briskly in and out from the moment Norah arrived, early the next morning.

She brought Rowdy his breakfast tray and found Robbins sitting behind the desk, working at the computer. A middle-aged woman with her dark hair in a tight chignon sat at a typewriter. No one seemed to notice Norah—least of all Rowdy, who was issuing orders like a general from his headquarters.

"I hope I'm not interrupting anything," Norah said, not bothering to restrain the sarcasm as she set down his breakfast tray.

"Norah." Rowdy's eyes lit up and he laid the file he was scanning aside. Horn-rimmed reading glasses were perched at the end of his nose; they only made him look more attractive.

"I brought your breakfast."

"I don't suppose you have any more of those blueberry muffins, do you?"

"I might."

"But it's going to cost me, right?"

"Not exactly." She'd read over the notes the night staff had left regarding Rowdy and learned he'd been on the phone all hours of the night. He'd called her, of course, but that had been much earlier in the evening.

She took the thermometer from its slot and stuck it under his tongue.

"I haven't got a fever! Why do you insist on taking my temperature all hours of the day and night?" he fussed when she was through.

She made the notation, and then reached for his wrist. "You were on the phone for nearly eight hours straight."

"Jealous?" He wiggled his eyebrows.

"I might be." She was far more concerned about his apparent lack of concern for his health.

"There were people I needed to talk to, people I had to reassure. By the way, did you see we got coverage on CNN? My plane crash put Orchard Valley on the map."

"I'm sure the mayor is thrilled."

"He offered me the keys to the city."

"Uncle Jack? He didn't!" Norah couldn't believe it.

Rowdy laughed boisterously. "No, he didn't, but he should have."

Norah finished taking his pulse and recorded the information.

"Now do I get those blueberry muffins or are you going to make me beg?"

Norah removed two cellophane-wrapped muffins from her sweater pockets. "Count your blessings, Cassidy. This is the last of the batch. My dad sent them to you with his best wishes."

"Bless him." Rowdy ignored the breakfast tray and unwrapped the muffins instead. "Meet Mrs. Emerich, my secretary. You remember Robbins, don't you?"

Norah smiled at both of Rowdy's employees.

"I know your sister, Valerie," Mrs. Emerich said, "a wonderful young woman. We all miss her dreadfully. Say hello for me, won't you?"

Norah nodded, carefully watching Rowdy. She wondered how he'd react to the mention of her sister's name. He didn't, at least not outwardly.

"Mr. Cassidy will need an hour later this morning," Norah told Robbins and Mrs. Emerich. "Dr. Silverman's scheduled to—"

"What time?" Rowdy demanded.

"The schedule says ten."

"He'll have to change it. I've got an interview with *Time* magazine at ten."

"Rowdy, you can't ask Dr. Silverman to rearrange his day because you're meeting with a magazine reporter."

"Why not? He'll understand. *Time*'s flying a reporter all the way from New York. I'm sure he won't mind waiting. He might even want to talk to the guy himself. I'll try to arrange it if I can."

"Kincade's reporting back to you at eleven," Mrs. Emerich reminded Rowdy.

"Damn, that's right. Listen," he said, directing his attention back to Norah. "Maybe it's best if you had Dr. Silverman check with Mrs. Emerich before he does whatever it is he needs to do."

Norah was too stunned, for a moment, to react. "Dr. Silverman will be here at ten," she said firmly. "If the reporter from *Time* magazine is here, then he'll need to wait outside the room like everyone else. This is a hospital, Mr. Cassidy. You may have managed to sweet-talk other people around here, but it won't work with me. Is that understood?"

A shocked silence fell after her words. Mrs. Emerich and Robbins both stood with their mouths open, as though they'd never heard anyone speak like this to their boss.

Rowdy's eyes went from dark to darker. "All right," he said finally, his voice sullen and angry.

Norah whirled around and left the room.

The results of Dr. Silverman's examination revealed signs of improvement. If his leg continued to mend, Rowdy could be discharged within two weeks. No one was more relieved than Norah.

The sooner Rowdy left, the better for her. Once he was gone, Norah felt confident her life would return to normal. Once Rowdy had left Orchard Valley, her heart could forget him.

They'd only kissed once, but it was enough—more than enough. She knew this was a dangerous man. Dangerous to her emotional well-being. More important, he was in love with her sister.

THREE DAYS LATER, on a Monday afternoon, Norah stopped in to find Rowdy resting. The room was silent, which was rare. Norah guessed that Mrs. Emerich and Robbins were out to lunch.

"I've got your medication," she said, spilling two capsules into the palm of his hand and giving him a small paper cup filled with water.

Rowdy swallowed down the pills.

He looked exhausted. It angered Norah that he insisted on working so hard, especially now when he needed to rest. He ran everyone around him ragged, yet he demanded twice as much of himself. She shook off her thoughts as she realized he was speaking to her.

"Did anyone ever tell you how much you look like an angel?" he asked.

"Just you."

He frowned. "You're very beautiful, Norah Bloomfield."

"And you're very tired."

"I must be," he said on the tail end of a yawn. "I wasn't going to say anything until later."

"Say what?" she prompted.

"About your angel face. You don't look a thing like Valerie."

Her sister's name went through her like an icy chill. The sister she loved and admired. The sister she'd always looked up to and idolized. Now, Norah could barely tolerate the sound of her own sister's name.

"Rest," she advised softly.

"Will you be here when I wake up?"

Norah hesitated. The ward was full, and she didn't have time to stay at his bedside, although it was exactly what she wanted to do.

"I'll be back later, when I'm finished with my shift."

"Promise?" His eyelids were drifting down even as he spoke.

"I promise." Impulsively she brushed the hair from his temple, letting her hand linger on his face. He was growing more important to her every moment, which frightened her terribly. She dreaded the day he'd be released, and in the same heartbeat willed it to hurry.

When Robbins and Mrs. Emerich returned half an hour later, Norah suggested they take the rest of the afternoon off. Rowdy would be furious, but she'd deal with him later. He was pushing himself too hard; he needed the rest.

Norah was sitting at his bedside when he awoke. He must have sensed she was there because he moved his head toward her and slowly smiled. "What time is it?"

"Four-thirty."

His eyes widened. "That late? But what about—"

"I gave them the afternoon off."

"Norah," he groaned. "I wish you hadn't. I was expecting several phone calls." He struggled to a half-sitting position and his gaze shot to the telephone. She stood and picked up the plug, dangling it from her fingers.

"You unplugged the phone?"

"As I explained earlier, you needed the rest."

Rowdy's mouth snapped shut and anger leaped into his eyes.

"As I've explained before, this is a hospital, Mr. Cassidy, not Grand Central Station. If the call was that important they'll try again tomorrow."

Rowdy pinched his lips closed. Norah suspected it was to prevent himself from unleashing some blistering invective.

"I do have one small piece of information for you, however," she said matter-of-factly.

Rowdy's eyes met hers, his expression inquiring.

"Valerie and Colby arrived home this afternoon."

Rowdy reached for the bar and sat upright, his face eager. His eyes sharpened the way they did whenever he felt strongly about something—or in this case, someone. "I need to see her right away," he said. "See what you can do to arrange it, would you?"

CHAPTER FIVE

"VALERIE IS just home from her honeymoon," Norah felt obliged to remind Rowdy. "You don't really expect me to drag her up here to visit you, do you?"

Rowdy seemed surprised by her question. "Of course I do. Valerie and I have unfinished business."

Norah's stomach tightened into hard knots. She'd been a fool, standing guard over Rowdy all afternoon, protecting him the way she had. Hurrying to his side the moment her shift ended... That had been her first mistake. She was determined not to make a second one. It wasn't Norah he wanted doting over him, it was Valerie.

"Valerie's married, Rowdy. Nothing's going to change that."

Pain flashed into his eyes and there was no mistaking the reason. Now, more than ever, Norah realized what a calamity it would be to risk her heart over a man in love with someone else. Especially when that someone happened to be her own sister.

Suddenly the mist cleared in Norah's mind. Rowdy had had her transferred to his floor, not out of any desire to be near her but to have a source of information about Valerie. Even the kiss, the one she'd treasured, had been nothing but a ploy.

With her heart aching, Norah walked around to the other side of his bed, being careful to avoid the office equipment positioned in every available space.

"I never asked you what you expected to accomplish when you flew into Orchard Valley. I assume you were hoping to do more than celebrate Valerie and Colby's happiness."

"Hell, yes," Rowdy admitted with an abrupt laugh, "I had to be sure Valerie knew what she was doing."

"You *couldn't* have believed Valerie would cancel the wedding!"

"That was something I had to find out. Everyone has their price."

His words stunned Norah. "You really think that, don't you?"

"Why shouldn't I? It works. I didn't want to lose Valerie, but at the same time I wasn't willing to give her what she wanted. So I gambled. She took me at face value, unfortunately, and I lost, but I might not have, except for the plane crash."

Norah shook her head. "What do you mean, you weren't willing to give Valerie what she wanted? What was that?"

"Marriage."

If she'd been shocked before, Norah was completely astounded now. She needed to sit down before her legs gave out and sank, speechless, into the bedside chair. The man was mad. He apparently believed Valerie had contrived her engagement to Colby with the intention of prompting Rowdy into a wedding proposal.

"I'm not the marrying kind, Norah. Valerie must have known that. I can't say we ever actually talked about it, but I figure anyone who's worked with me knows I don't have time for a wife or family. Don't need 'em."

"I'm sure that's true," Norah said tightly.

Rowdy studied her closely. "Are you upset about something?"

"No. Yes!" She jumped to her feet. "Let me see if I understand you correctly. You want me to bring my sister to you, but as far as I can tell, your reasons for wanting to see her are entirely self-serving. You don't care about Valerie and Colby. The only person you care about is yourself."

He hesitated and his brows knitted together as he mulled over her words. "I'm not going to tell you about the nature of my business with your sister, if that's what you're asking."

"You don't have to," she said coldly, ignoring the intense pain she felt. "I know everything I need to. If you want to talk to Valerie, I suggest you draft someone else to arrange it."

VALERIE, tanned and relaxed after her honeymoon, was potting red geraniums on the sun-washed patio outside her house—the house she and Colby had bought near the outskirts of Orchard Valley. Norah was sipping iced tea, sitting under the shade of a large umbrella, watching her sister work. The pungent scent of freshly squeezed lemons drifted on the breeze. The afternoon was growing hot and humid, but neither Norah nor Valerie seemed to notice.

"What happened between you and Rowdy Cassidy when you flew back to Texas?" Norah asked.

Valerie paused, her hands deep in the potting soil. "We didn't part on good terms, but I'm afraid it was my fault."

Norah said nothing, but her expression must have revealed her skepticism.

"I'm serious," Valerie insisted.

Norah hesitated before she said, "I was sorry you had to hear about Rowdy's accident on your wedding day. Dad and Steffie and I weren't sure what to do. We didn't tell you right away because you had so much on your mind."

"Don't worry. Dad already talked to me about it. You did the right thing."

Norah's hands closed around the tea glass. She gazed into the distance for a moment, then said in a small voice, "He's in love with you."

With one wrist, Valerie tipped the large straw hat farther back on her head, laughing softly. "Rowdy might think he is, but believe me, Norah, he isn't. However, offering him my letter of resignation didn't help the situation."

She pressed the moist potting soil carefully around a geranium. "I underestimated Rowdy's ego," she explained. "He's a man who doesn't like to lose. He hasn't had much practice at it, and that's the problem. He's so wealthy he can buy anything he wants, and to complicate matters, he can charm a worm right out of an apple when he puts his mind to it."

"I—I know it isn't any of my business," Norah said, feeling as though she was invading her sister's privacy "but what happened when you told him about Colby?"

Valerie straightened, shaking the earth from her hands. "I didn't immediately mention I was engaged, which was a mistake. The first thing I brought up was my feasibility study on expanding CHIPS into the Pacific Northwest. I was eager to show Rowdy all my research. I presented the project in a favorable light, and I convinced him now was the time to do it.

"Before Rowdy knew I was engaged to Colby," Valerie continued, "he committed himself to the project. That thrilled me, of course, because I wanted to be the one to head it up."

"He's very savvy when it comes to business, isn't he? I mean, he's even working from his hospital bed."

"Rowdy's very talented," Valerie agreed. "But he's stubborn and he likes to have his own way."

"I've noticed," Norah said, grinning.

Valerie laughed. "I'll bet you have."

"Anyway, get back to your story."

"Well, I pushed the project, and he gave it the go-ahead—until I told him I wanted to run it myself. Rowdy said he'd rather I stayed in Texas and worked with him. He reached for my hands then and I had the feeling he was about to say something...romantic. I'm only grateful he noticed the engagement ring first. And that was when I told him about Colby."

Norah's heart went out to Rowdy. "He must have been shocked."

"He was, and angry, too." Valerie's face tightened at the memory. "He told me he thought I was too smart to let myself fall for that love-and-marriage stuff. He said that marrying Colby would be a disaster for my career." Valerie's gaze skidded self-consciously away from Norah. "I—I don't know if I ever said anything to you about Rowdy, but I was a little sweet on him before I met Colby. When I first got home, just before Dad's surgery, I'd started to believe he might feel the same way toward me."

"He does."

Valerie laughed and shook her head. "I hope I'm around to watch what happens when Rowdy actually does fall in love. It's going to knock that poor cowboy for one heck of a wallop."

"Go on," Norah encouraged.

"Where was I . . . oh, yes. When Rowdy discovered I was definitely engaged to Colby, he tried to talk me out of it. He even claimed it was his duty as my friend and employer to do whatever he could to keep me from making such a terrible mistake."

"He doesn't lack impudence, does he?"

"Not in the least," Valerie said with a grin. "He felt that in view of my recent poor judgment, Oregon was the worst place for me to be, so he offered the expansion project to Earl Robbins. In that case, I told him, I didn't have any choice. So I typed up my resignation and handed it to him. He seemed to think I was bluffing. He accepted the resignation, but blithely informed me that I would recognize the error of my ways and come back to CHIPS. I won't, though, not if it means leaving Oregon."

"Did it frighten you to quit like that? You never said. All I can remember is a comment you made about taking an extended vacation until after the honeymoon."

Valerie nodded thoughtfully. "For the first while, I had the wedding plans to keep me occupied, but I soon had that under control. Colby's been wonderfully encouraging, and we've discussed a number of possibilities. I've got my application in with a couple of firms in Portland, but I don't feel a burning need to find a job right away. To be honest, I'm enjoying this time off. It feels good to plant flowers and sit in the sunshine."

"What do you think you'd like to do?" Norah asked.

"Colby and I have discussed the idea of starting a consulting business out of the house. That way I could set my own hours and work when I wanted, which appeals to me. But I'm going to do some research into it before I make any firm decisions. For now I'm content."

"Rowdy wants to see you," Norah said abruptly, her voice unintentionally sharp. "He's been pestering me ever since he heard you and Colby were back."

Valerie's hands stilled. "I supposed I should go visit him. It's the least I can do."

Norah wasn't so sure.

"DID YOU HEAR?" Rowdy asked when Norah saw him next.

"About what?"

"My stock's up two full points, and the price has remained steady all week."

To Norah's way of thinking, it must be agony to live a life controlled by the Dow Jones Industrial Average, but she didn't comment. "Congratulations."

Rowdy watched her closely. "Are you upset about our last talk?" He glanced at his two employees and kept his voice low.

"Of course not," Norah lied. "Why should I be? You want to talk to my sister, and that's perfectly understandable. As you reminded me, it isn't any of my business."

She walked around the end of his bed, removed the chart and made the necessary notations.

"I shouldn't have been so brusque."

That was only one in a long list of offenses, but Norah didn't bother to say so.

"You haven't been in to see me as often," he said next.

"I've been too busy."

"Even for me?" He used a hurt little-boy tone and Norah couldn't resist smiling.

"You'll be happy to know I saw Valerie yesterday afternoon," she went on, not daring to look up, afraid of what she might read in his eyes. "I explained that you wanted to see her and she said she'd be in sometime in the next few days."

"I hope it's soon because Dr. Silverman's given the go-ahead to get me out of this rigging. I'm scheduled to be released on Friday."

Norah waited a moment, finding it difficult to identify her reactions. She was beginning to know this man, faults and all—and despite everything, she was crazy about him.

Their views often clashed, but that didn't change her feelings. And his employees, at least the ones she'd met, were deeply committed to him. It took a lot more than money to inspire such loyalty.

At the same time, Norah recognized how dangerous it was for her to be around Rowdy much longer. He'd evoked a wide range of emotions: anger, outrage, laughter, pride and others that weren't as simple to define. It would be so easy to fall in love with him.... The mere thought terrified her.

"Aren't you going to say something?" Rowdy asked.

"We'll miss you around here," she said, putting on a false smile. "Good grief, what'll we do for excitement now?"

"You'll think of something," he assured her.

"No doubt, but I don't think Orchard Valley will ever be the same."

"Take a note, Mrs. Emerich," Rowdy insisted, keeping his gaze focused on Norah. "Small Oregon towns are no longer on my agenda. They're a risk to my health."

"I hope you understand that once you're discharged from here, you can't just go back to your regular work schedule," Norah pointed out.

"So I heard," Rowdy said, frowning. "I'm going to be stuck with several months of physical therapy."

"Don't shortchange yourself on that, Rowdy. You're going to need it."

He wasn't too pleased about this additional treatment, Norah knew. Then she sighed; he hadn't even left the hospital and already she was worrying about him. Oh, yes, she was going to miss him.

He must have seen the regret in her eyes because his own grew dark and serious. "Can you come back later?" he asked in a low voice. "Tonight. There's something I need to ask you."

Norah hesitated. "All right," she finally whispered.

"Around seven," he said briskly, "and don't eat dinner."

NORAH WASN'T SURE what to expect that evening. She wore a sleeveless pale pink dress, the shade similar to her bridesmaid's dress. On impulse she'd put on the dangling gold earrings that had belonged to her mother. She wore them only for special occasions....

Her father didn't ask where she was going, but his complacent expression told Norah he knew. "You look absolutely beautiful," he said as she came down the stairs. "You have a wonderful evening, now."

"I'm sure I will." She half expected him to interrogate her, but he didn't even ask one question.

"I won't wait up for you."

"Have a good evening then, Dad."

"I will, sweetheart, I will," he said and then he did the oddest thing. He raised his head, eyes closed, and mumbled something she couldn't hear.

When Norah arrived at the hospital, she discovered that Rowdy had transformed his room into a romantic bower. The window shades were closed, allowing only glimmers of the evening light inside. Candles flickered from a linen-covered table, and half a dozen vases of fresh flowers were strategically placed throughout the room. The office furniture he'd had delivered was pushed as far against the wall as possible. A bottle of white wine was chilling in a silver bucket. Soft, lilting music played in the background. For an instant she wondered if she'd stepped into a dream, a fantasy.

"My goodness." The words escaped on a whisper of awe.

Rowdy wasn't wearing a hospital gown, but had dressed in a black Western shirt with string tie and a pair of jeans slit along one side to accommodate his cast. The effort he'd made touched her deeply.

"I hope you're hungry," he said, with a boyishly pleased grin.

"I'm starved," she assured him, walking over to the bed. The room seemed so private, so cozy, but she didn't hesitate. "What's on the menu?"

"Examine it for yourself. It only got here a minute ago."

Norah lifted the domed lid over the two plates and found crab-and-shrimp-stuffed sole, a wild rice pilaf and fresh broccoli with thin slivers of carrot. Two huge slices of strawberry-covered cheesecake rested next to the wineglasses.

"I had the chef check out the cholesterol count, if you're interested."

"Oh, Rowdy, you amaze me."

"Somehow or another I knew you'd swoon for cheesecake."

Norah laughed, because it was true, and because she was almost giddy with excitement—and happiness.

"Now pick up the gift that's on the edge of the table and open it."

Norah found the small, brightly wrapped box and carried it to his bedside. She raised questioning eyes to his. "What's this?"

"You'll have to open it and see."

Norah frowned. "I didn't do anything to deserve this." She was only one of the medical professionals who'd assisted Rowdy in his recovery.

"Quit arguing with me and open the package," Rowdy instructed. She finally nodded and carefully tore away the paper, uncovering a velvet box with the name of an expensive Portland jeweler etched in a gold flourish across the top.

She glanced at him again, still puzzled.

"Open it," he said again. "I picked it out myself."

Hardly daring to breathe, Norah lifted the lid and discovered a sapphire-and-diamond necklace, exquisite in its simplicity. She released her breath on a soft sigh of appreciation. "Oh, Rowdy... I've never seen anything this lovely."

"Then you like it?"

"Yes, but I could never accept it...."

"Nonsense. Turn around—I want to see it on you." Before she could protest further, he removed the necklace from its plush bed and opened the clasp. He held it with both hands, prepared to place it around her neck.

Norah pivoted slowly around and pressed her hand to the necklace when he positioned it against her throat. She'd never been given something so valuable or so beautiful.

"This is my way of thanking you for everything you did for me, Norah."

"But I—"

"You were my saving grace," he cut in, obviously impatient with her objections. "Arguing with you was the one thing that got me through those early days. You were generous and unselfish, even though I behaved like a spoiled brat. I'm grateful, and I want to express my gratitude."

"Well, then, I accept. And . . . and I thank you very much." Norah felt tears gather in the corners of her eyes. "Shall we open the wine?" she asked briskly, not wanting Rowdy to know how deeply his generosity had affected her. She lifted the wine bottle from its icy bucket and hesitated. "Are you sure you can cross alcohol with your medication?"

"I have Dr. Silverman's permission. If you don't believe me, you can call him yourself. He left his number with me in case you had any concerns."

Rowdy had thought of everything. Grinning, Norah handed him the bottle and corkscrew and watched as he deftly opened the Chablis. Norah brought over their glasses; he sampled the wine, then filled both goblets.

"We'd better eat before the fish gets cold," he said. Norah returned to the dinner table for his plate. His own place setting was neatly arranged on top of the nightstand.

"Next time we have dinner together, I'll be sitting across the table from you," he promised.

Norah sat down and spread the crisp linen napkin across her lap. In all her years of hospital work, she'd never seen anything like this. Of course, she'd never known anyone like Rowdy Cassidy, either.

"This is fabulous," Norah said after the first bite. She closed her eyes and savored the wonderful blend of seafood, sole and lightly seasoned sauce.

"Save room for dessert."

Norah eyed the huge fresh strawberries on the cheesecake. "No problem there." She felt a bit silly sitting at the table alone and after her second bite, got to her feet and carried her plate to the nightstand.

"It'll do me good to stand up and eat," she told him. "I'll have more room for the cheesecake that way."

Rowdy grinned. The room was growing dark as the sun set, a warm, intimate darkness, and the candle flames seemed to dance to the soft music.

It took Norah an instant to realize they'd both stopped eating. Slowly, his eyes holding hers, Rowdy pushed the nightstand away so there was nothing between them. His hands on her waist, he guided her to the bed.

"Sit next to me," he whispered.

She glanced at his leg, needing to gauge the effect her weight would have on the pulleys.

"I'll be fine."

Norah carefully sat on the edge of the bed. Her gaze was level with Rowdy's.

"No wonder I thought you were an angel," he whispered. The husky pitch of his voice thrilled her. "You're so beautiful...."

No man had evoked such emotions in her before. She didn't *want* to feel any of these things, not with a man like Rowdy, but she couldn't stop herself.

He captured her face between his hands and rubbed the side of his thumb across her moist mouth. She sensed a barely restrained urgency in him, and still he didn't kiss her. Excitement raced through her veins.

"Rowdy." His name became a whispered plea.

She wasn't completely sure what she wanted from him; he seemed to understand better than she did herself. He reached for her and wrapped her unceremoniously in his arms. His mouth claimed hers, and whatever defenses she'd erected against him in the past two weeks, whatever doubts she'd harbored, were banished under the onslaught of his kiss.

Just when Norah thought she might faint with the exhilaration of his touch, Rowdy trailed his mouth across her cheek to the scented hollow of her throat. His tongue made moist, tantalizing forays against her warm skin. She sighed and sagged against him, weak and without will.

"I've wanted to do that from the first time I saw you," he whispered huskily. "When you stood there, in that long pink dress—like an angel." He groaned and shook his head. "I've tried to be patient, tried to wait until I was out of this blasted cast, but I couldn't. Not a moment longer."

Norah buried her hands in his thick, dark hair and spread eager kisses over his face. She'd wanted him, too. Badly. So badly that she'd been afraid to admit it, even to herself.

He kissed her again, a deeper kiss this time. "I thought I'd go crazy these past few weeks," he murmured. "I've thought about nothing except holding you again, kissing you again. You've been so close— and yet so far away from me."

Norah felt warm and weightless in his arms. He kissed her with even greater insistence, and it seemed that she'd never experienced anything this good in her entire life. Tears of joy flooded her eyes as she tipped her head back to grant him easier exploration of her throat. Shivers of excitement danced over her skin and she gave a deep, deep sigh.

"Come to Texas with me." The words were low and urgent. He held her tightly against him as though he never wanted to let her go.

It took a moment for the words to sink past the fog of longing that blurred her thoughts. "Come to Texas with you?" she repeated. Slowly she eased herself from his embrace, her eyes seeking out his. Her heart went wild with expectant hope.

"As my personal nurse."

Norah wasn't sure she'd heard him correctly. His nurse. He wanted her as his nurse. For one soaring moment she'd assumed, she'd hoped, that he wanted her for herself. For always. She'd dreamed he wanted her to— A warm shade of pink blossomed in her cheeks as she realized what a fool she'd been. He'd told her before that he wasn't interested in marriage or family life. If he hadn't been willing to marry Valerie, whom he loved, then he certainly wasn't interested in her. CHIPS was his life, his reason for being. She'd witnessed it herself, the way all his energy, all his emotion, was dedicated to the success of his company.

"I'm going to need someone to look after me," he continued, reaching for her fingers and squeezing lightly, "to make sure I don't do more than I should. Someone who'll bully me into taking care of myself. Will you fly back with me, Norah?" He raised her hand to his lips and kissed her palm. "I need you."

How she'd longed to hear those words from Rowdy, but she'd wanted them to mean something very different.

It didn't take Norah more than a second to decide. "I can't leave Orchard Valley."

His gaze narrowed. "Why not?"

"It's my home. I've lived here all my life. My father's here, my job is here, my family. Everything that's important to me is here."

"You'll be back in a little while. I shouldn't need you for more than . . . say, a couple of months."

Norah backed away from him but her feet felt as if they'd been weighted down with cement. The little she'd eaten of her dinner rested like a concrete block in the pit of her stomach. Rowdy had arranged everything that evening in an effort to convince her to leave with him. As his nurse. Nothing more.

An overwhelming weariness came over her.

"Reconsider," he pleaded. "I promise you it won't be for long."

Norah shook her head. As far as she was concerned there wasn't anything to reconsider.

His mouth tightened with unconcealed irritation. "I'll make it worth your while. I'll triple whatever the hospital's paying you now."

She didn't doubt it. But financial concerns weren't what held her back. "I'm . . . pleased that you'd ask me, but it wouldn't work, Rowdy."

"Why the hell not?" he demanded. "I'm going to need someone and I want *you*."

"But I'm not for sale."

"I didn't mean it like that," he flared, running his hand roughly through his hair. Norah could feel the frustration in him. It might have been petty of her, but she felt a fleeting satisfaction. She wanted him to taste her own disappointment.

"I don't know what it is with you Bloomfield women," he grumbled, pushing the nightstand back into place. "There's no pleasing you, is there?" He lowered his voice. "I never met a pair of more head-strong women in my life."

"You'll do just fine without me." She was slowly recovering from the influence of his touch. Valerie was right; Rowdy Cassidy knew how to stack a deck in his favor. Knowing she was attracted to him, he'd attempted to sway her decision with wine and a luscious meal—and kisses.

Rowdy sliced his cheesecake with enough force to crack the plate. "Damn fool woman," he muttered.

Norah couldn't help laughing, despite the dull ache in her heart. "If you want, I'll recommend a reputable agency that provides nurses for private care."

"I don't want anyone but you." He stabbed a strawberry and poised it in front of his mouth. "You still haven't forgiven me for being honest, have you?"

"About what?"

"My feelings toward Valerie. I knew when I told you I'd regret it, and by heaven I was right."

"This doesn't have anything to do with my sister."

"Then why won't you fly back to Texas with me? I've got a private jet coming in. You won't lack for luxury, Norah, and if you're worried about propriety, I'll have Mrs. Emerich move in with us."

"That isn't it."

"I should have guessed you'd be this stubborn. It runs in the family, doesn't it?"

"It most certainly does."

Rowdy leaned over and flipped a switch that turned off the music. "I didn't think this...dinner would work. Mrs. Emerich was the one who suggested it."

Norah walked across the room and opened the blinds. "The evening's too lovely to shut out."

Rowdy folded his arms and muttered something she couldn't hear.

There was a polite knock at the door.

"Come in," Rowdy barked.

The door slowly opened and Valerie Bloomfield Winston stepped inside.

CHAPTER SIX

"I'M NOT INTERRUPTING anything, am I?" Valerie
asked. She remained on the threshold, oddly hesitant
and unsure.

"Of course you're not." Norah recovered enough
to speak first. She felt as though she were five years
old again, caught with her hand in the cookie jar.

Rowdy merely closed his eyes—in resignation, Norah supposed, at the prospect of facing another
Bloomfield. "You might as well come in," he invited
ungraciously.

"If you'd rather I stopped by another time..."
Valerie suggested, glancing at them doubtfully. "It
wouldn't be any problem." Her gaze caught Norah's,
who was convinced her cheeks had flamed a fiery red.

"Don't worry," Rowdy muttered, "you weren't interrupting a thing."

"Rowdy asked me to accompany him back to
Texas...as his nurse," Norah explained, her tongue
stumbling over the words. She gestured weakly toward the elaborately set table and silver wine bucket.

"Ah..." Her sister was smart enough to figure out
what had happened.

"Have you decided to take the job?" Valerie asked,
looking at Norah.

"No," Norah said emphatically.

Rowdy frowned—again. "I should have known she'd be as stubborn as you. Norah doesn't want the job, even at ten times what she earns here. She wants blood."

"It's time I left," Norah said, reaching for her purse. "I'm sure you two have a lot to talk about."

"Don't go," Valerie countered smoothly. "Fact is, I'd rather you stayed." She lifted the wine bottle from the silver bucket and read the label. Apparently she was impressed, because her eyebrows arched. "I see you didn't spare any expense."

"Are you here to gloat or do you want to talk?" Rowdy demanded irritably.

"He gets feisty," Valerie warned Norah under her breath, "when he can't have his own way."

"Quit talking about me as if I wasn't here." Rowdy snapped. He readjusted himself, using the triangular bar to straighten himself and shift positions. "You and I need to clear the air, Valerie Bloomfield."

"I suspect we do," Valerie agreed. "And the name's Winston now."

Norah knew she should leave, but she felt rooted to the floor. Her eyes strayed from Valerie to Rowdy, wondering how much of his feelings he'd dare reveal to her sister. He'd loved her enough to fly to Orchard Valley, but even now she wasn't completely sure what his intentions had been.

"Despite everything I told you, you went ahead and married Carlton, anyway," he muttered.

"Colby," Valerie and Norah corrected simultaneously.

"Whoever," Rowdy returned irritably. "You married him!" In response, Valerie raised her left hand and wiggled her ring finger.

"You can kiss your career goodbye, but you already know that, don't you?" Rowdy said. "I've seen it happen a thousand times, brilliant careers flushed down the drain and all in the name of love. As far as I'm concerned, it's a bunch of hogwash."

Valerie didn't say anything for a long moment. "At one time, working for you and CHIPS was the most important thing in my life."

"See?" Rowdy shouted, looking at Norah and pointing toward Valerie, "it's happening already! And she's only been married, what? Two weeks."

"Three," Valerie inserted.

"Three weeks and already her mind is warped."

Valerie laughed, and Norah found her amusement somehow reassuring. "Love tends to do that to a person."

"Then heaven help us all." Rowdy crossed his arms over his muscular chest and turned his head to gaze steadfastly out the window. "You were one of the best," he finally said, still not looking directly at the two women. "It's a shame to lose you."

"As I recall, you didn't leave me much choice. You wouldn't give me the job I wanted, and you knew I wouldn't stay in Texas."

He winced and Norah saw a flash of regret in his eyes, a reappearance of the pain she'd noticed whenever Valerie's name was mentioned. Norah experienced a pang of her own, knowing that the man she loved cared so deeply for her sister.

"I...may have acted a bit hastily," Rowdy said with a contriteness he didn't bother to conceal. "Robbins is a good man, don't get me wrong, but he doesn't have the gut instincts you do when it comes to making a go of this expansion project. He took the assignment because I asked him to, but if the truth be known, you were always the person for the job. Not Robbins."

Valerie paced the room in silence; Norah almost demanded her sister say something to ease the tension. Val had told her only a little of the confrontation that had taken place between her and Rowdy, but she knew an apology when she heard one. Valerie's former employer was trying to mend fences.

"What are you saying, Rowdy? That you want me back with CHIPS for the expansion project?"

"That's exactly what I'm saying."

"I'll never be the businesswoman I was, as you've already pointed out. Marriage has ruined me, you know."

Rowdy's face relaxed with the beginnings of a smile. "There might be some hope for you yet. Once you're with CHIPS again, we'll be able to work on your attitude. Of course it'll take time, training and patience, but Robbins and I should be able to whip you into shape."

Valerie didn't say anything. Norah stared at her sister, willing her to answer Rowdy. Willing her to recognize what it had cost his pride to make that offer. If Valerie didn't appreciate how difficult it was for him to admit he'd been wrong, then Norah did. Surely Val understood what he was really saying!

"I'm flattered."

For a moment Rowdy didn't react, then he slammed one hand against the other and swore under his breath. "You're going to turn me down, aren't you? I know that obstinate look of yours. Apparently it runs in the family." He was glaring at Norah as he spoke.

"I'm not committing myself either way just yet. The project will consume every waking minute for months, and I'm not sure that's what I want," Valerie told him honestly.

"You were willing enough to take it on before," Rowdy argued. "What's so different?"

"I'm married. I have responsibilities to someone other than myself. I didn't fully understand what that entailed when I first talked to you, but I know now, and I'm not willing to let CHIPS control my life. Not anymore."

"What do you intend to do? Stay barefoot and pregnant the rest of your life?"

"Rowdy!" Norah chastised, offended that he'd talk to her sister that way. He ignored her, staring combatively at Valerie.

"Colby and I do eventually want children, but I was toying with the idea of starting my own business."

"Software?" His dark eyes became sharp as steel. It went without saying that Valerie could be keen competition if she chose to be.

"No," she said with amusement. "Consulting. I'll set my own hours, and I'll train others, so once the business expands—or I do—it won't be unmanageable." She grinned at Rowdy. "I'll be able to combine work and a family in whatever way suits me best."

He nodded. "It makes sense, damn good sense."

Valerie smiled cheerfully. "That wasn't so hard to admit, now was it?"

"No," he agreed. His eyes softened as he studied Valerie. He seemed to have forgotten Norah was in the room. "I was a fool to ever let you leave Texas. We might have had something good between us. Something really good."

Valerie's gaze met his, and in it Norah read so many things. Her sister greatly admired Rowdy Cassidy, but the respect she held for him could never compare to the love she shared with Colby.

"I know, I know," Rowdy said with a weak smile. "It was too little, too late. Well, I want to wish you and Carlton the very best."

"Colby," Valerie and Norah reminded him, and all three burst out laughing.

"YOU'RE HOME earlier than I expected," David Bloomfield said when Norah walked in the house an hour later. He was standing in the doorway of his den, dressed in flannel robe and slippers. A magazine lay on the arm of his favorite chair. "I was just going to make myself a cup of hot chocolate. Care to join me?"

"Sure." She trailed her father into the kitchen. "Where's Steffie?"

"She went out to dinner with Charles. I don't think she'll be home for a while."

It didn't seem possible that Steffie and Charles would be married in two weeks' time. They'd decided to have a ceremony next to the apple orchard, with the reception to follow on the huge front lawn. It would be a relaxed affair with plenty of fun, food and laughter.

"Did you enjoy yourself?" David asked in that deceptively casual way of his. Norah knew her father well enough to recognize his interest as more than idle curiosity. He was eager to hear the details. And tonight, Norah was just as eager to talk.

"I had dinner with Rowdy this evening. He had the meal catered." While she was talking, Norah took a saucepan from the cupboard and set it on the stove to heat the milk for their cocoa.

Her father leaned back in his chair, assuming a relaxed pose.

"Dad," Norah said, holding the milk carton in her hand and gazing absently into space. "If you had the opportunity to travel for...a job, would you take it?"

"That depends. Where would I be traveling to?"

"A long way from home—but not too far. Texas, actually. But it wouldn't be for pleasure—or not exactly. It'd be on the pretense of a job, but not a taxing one." Rowdy might claim he needed her, but Norah knew better. She'd end up twiddling her thumbs ninety percent of the time. Even if she did insist that Rowdy slow down his pace, he wasn't likely to listen to her. As far as she could see, her presence would serve no useful purpose, other than entertainment. Hadn't he said he enjoyed arguing with her?

"Am I to understand Rowdy has asked you to go with him when he leaves Orchard Valley?"

"As his private nurse," Norah explained, pouring milk into the pan. "It'd only be for a few weeks."

"You're not sure what you want, are you? The temptation to go with him is there, but you don't feel good about doing it. Am I right?"

Norah was a little surprised at how easily her father had identified her dilemma, but she merely shrugged in reply.

"You like Rowdy Cassidy, don't you?" her father questioned softly.

Norah added cocoa to the warm milk and stirred briskly. "He's stubborn as a mule, and I swear I've never known anyone more egotistical. His arrogance is beyond explaining and he—"

"But you like him." Her father spoke again, and this time his words were a statement and not a question.

Norah's hand stilled. "I think there must be something wrong with me, Dad. Rowdy's in love with Valerie—he might as well have come right out and said it."

"You're sure about that?"

Norah wasn't sure of anything. Not now. For one thing, it just didn't make sense that Rowdy could hold her and kiss her the way he had if he was really in love with her sister.

"Valerie came to see him . . . while I was there. He asked her to come and work for him again." She turned back to the stove and resumed stirring. Her feelings about what had taken place between Rowdy and her sister hadn't sorted themselves out in her mind yet. What did his offer to Valerie really mean? Was he so desperate to have her back in his life that he was willing to ignore her marriage to Colby? A flashing pain cut through her at the thought.

"Are you sure you're not mistaking regret for love?" her father asked gently. "Rowdy and Valerie had worked together a heck of a long time. Her engagement came as a shock to him. My feeling about their last confrontation—when Val flew to Houston—was that they both said things they later regretted."

"Valerie didn't turn down his offer, but she did ask for time to think it over. She refused to make a commitment either way." Norah poured the steaming cocoa into mugs and carried them to the table. "But you know, I think that was exactly what Rowdy expected from her. He was angry at first, but I had the impression it was more for show than anything."

David chuckled, then sipped his hot chocolate. "My guess is that being thwarted by two of my girls in one evening came as something of a shock to the boy."

Norah paused. "How'd you know I turned him down?"

David shrugged. "I just do. I'm not exactly sure why, but I knew you had. Are you having second thoughts now?"

"And third. Earlier I was so sure I'd made the right decision—and now I'm not."

Knowing that Rowdy would be out of her life in a matter of days had given her pause. His reaction was apparently the same. He didn't need a private nurse, and even if she'd accepted his generous offer, she wouldn't serve any useful purpose. She'd be there to provide entertainment... Norah gave a deep, heartfelt sigh.

Her father pointed at the sapphire-and-diamond necklace. "Is that new?" he asked.

Norah's hand went to her throat and she nodded. "Rowdy gave it to me—as a bribe I suspect. I suppose I should return it to him. Actually, I'd forgotten I had it on. It's beautiful, isn't it?"

"Very. If you want my advice about the necklace, keep it. Rowdy never intended it as a bribe. He's truly grateful for everything you've done." He swallowed down the last of his chocolate and stood.

"How can you be so certain?" Norah wanted to know.

Her father hesitated, frowning slightly. "I just am." With that, he turned and walked away.

WHEN NORAH ARRIVED at the hospital late the following morning, Rowdy's bed was empty.

She walked into the room and for a moment was too stunned to move. After spending a restless night weighing the pros and cons of his offer, she felt she had to talk to him again, even if it meant visiting the hospital on her day off.

"Looking for someone?" Rowdy asked from behind her.

She whirled around to discover him sitting in a wheelchair, his leg extended and supported. "When did this happen?"

"Only a few minutes ago. Damn, but it feels good to be out of that bed."

Norah laughed and knew immediately what she wanted to do. "I imagine it does. Stay here a minute. I'll be right back, I promise." She checked in at the nurses' station, scanned Rowdy's chart and quickly returned to his room.

"What are you doing now?" he asked when she stepped behind the wheelchair and began to push him down the hallway. "Hey, where are we going? Not so fast," he muttered. "I'm getting dizzy... Besides, I want a chance to take in the view. All I've seen for weeks are the four same walls."

"Just be patient," Norah said, enjoying herself. Finding his bed empty had sent her into a tailspin. But once she'd realized what she should do, she'd experienced an overwhelming sense of relief. She was almost giddy with it.

"Are you kidnapping me?" he joked, when she backed him into the elevator. "It sounds a bit kinky, but I could go for that."

"Hush now," she said, smiling at a visiting priest who shared the elevator with them.

"I always knew you were crazy about me," Rowdy continued. "But I never realized how much."

"Rowdy!" She rolled her eyes, then looked in the priest's direction. "You'll have to excuse him, Father, he's just spent the past few weeks tied to a bed."

"So I see." The priest glanced toward Rowdy's right leg.

"There were... other complications," Norah said with an exaggerated sigh.

"Poor fellow. I'll be saying a prayer for you, young man."

"Thank you, Father," Rowdy said so seriously that it was all Norah could do not to break into giggles.

The morning was gorgeous. The sun was shining, but the earth remained fresh with dew and the scent of blooming flowers drifted past on a warm breeze.

Robins, goldfinches and bluebirds flitted about, chirping exuberantly.

Following a paved pathway, Norah pushed the wheelchair to a small knoll of rosebushes that over-looked the town. Orchard Valley lay spread out like an intricate quilt below them. Norah stepped forward to watch Rowdy's face when he saw her home.

For a long moment he said nothing. "It's a peace-ful sort of place, isn't it?"

"Yes," she said quietly. "People still care about one another here." She sat on a stone bench and breathed in the fresh morning air.

"Is this the reason you won't come with me?" Rowdy asked, gazing out over the town. "Because you don't want to leave Orchard Valley?"

"No," she answered honestly. "You're the rea-son."

"Me?" He wore a puzzled, hurt look. "It's the necklace, isn't it? You assume because I gave you a gift that I was asking you to be more than my nurse."

"No," she told him quickly. "That didn't even cross my mind. It's so many other things." She sighed and leaned back, resting her hands on the sun-warmed bench. "I've never been more impressed by anyone than by you, Rowdy Cassidy. Your business judg-ment, your decisiveness, your sheer nerve. Your kindness, too. Just when I'm convinced you're the most egotistical, vain man I've ever known, you do something wonderful that completely baffles me."

"Like what?"

"Like offering my sister her job back."

"I'd behaved like a fool with Valerie. We both knew it, and it was up to me to make amends. I suppose you think it's because I'm carrying a torch for her." He paused as if he were trying to decipher her expression. "But I swear that isn't the case. If you must know, I felt cheated when Valerie returned to Houston engaged. I'd missed her like hell for all those weeks, and I was looking forward to having her back. Next thing I know, she announces she's going to marry some doctor." He shook his head. "I'll tell you, it felt like a slap in the face when I heard about Colby."

A weight seemed to lift from Norah's shoulders. Impulsively, she leaned forward just enough to brush her lips against his cheek.

Perplexed, Rowdy raised his hand to his jaw. "What was that for?"

"A reward for getting Colby's name right." She smiled in relief. Rowdy's resentment toward Valerie's husband was gone and, however reluctantly, he'd accepted both the situation and the man. She also had a glimmer of insight into his feelings: his pride had taken a severe battering. Rowdy was used to being in control, and suddenly—with Valerie—he wasn't. "Sorry," she said, "I didn't mean to interrupt you."

"Don't be so hasty." He folded his arms, relaxing in the warm sun. "What will you do if I say Colby's name three times in rapid succession?"

Norah smiled. "I don't know. I might go completely wild."

Rowdy laughed outright, then grew serious. "Damn, but I'm going to miss you."

Norah lowered her eyes as the dread filled her. "I'm going to miss you, too," she whispered.

He reached for her hands, covering them with his own. "Come with me, Norah," he asked her again.

"I'll work out something with the hospital. I'll buy the whole damn building if I have to, but I want you by my side."

The temptation was so strong that Norah briefly closed her eyes against the almost physical pull she experienced. "I . . . can't."

"Why?" he demanded, clearly exasperated. "I don't understand it. You want to come, I know you do, and I want you with me. Is that so difficult to understand?"

Norah pressed her hands against the sides of his face. He was so dear to her. When she said goodbye to him, she was sure a small part of her would die.

"Answer me," he pleaded.

Norah felt the emotion building in her, felt tears crowd into her eyes. "You need to understand something about me, Rowdy. Right now, you know me as a competent nurse, as Valerie's little sister, but you don't really *know* me. I have lots of friends and I like to go out, but basically I'm a homebody. Oh, I enjoy traveling now and again, but home is where my heart is. I love to bake and knit. Every year I plant a huge vegetable garden."

His expression revealed how mystified he was.

"I'm nothing like Valerie. She's so talented in ways I'm not."

"Do you think I've got the two of you confused in my mind?"

"No," she answered softly. "I just don't want you to think of me as her replacement."

His eyes widened and he slowly shook his head. "No, Norah, I swear to you that isn't the case."

"You don't need a nurse. You'll do fine if you use a bit of common sense. Once the cast is off, you'll require physical therapy for a while, but I won't be able to help you with that. I'm not trained for it."

"I like being with you," he said defensively. "Is that so wrong?"

"No."

"Then what exactly is the problem?"

"You don't know the kind of person I am...."

"That's what I'd like to find out," he argued, "if you'd give me half a chance and quit being so damn stubborn."

"I'm traditional and old-fashioned," she said, ignoring his outburst, "and...you're not. I'm the kind of woman who enjoys sitting by the fireplace and knitting at night. I'm not an adventurer, a risk-taker, like Valerie. I love my own familiar little world. And...and someday I want to marry and raise a family."

"I wanted to hire you as a nurse," Rowdy growled. "Next thing I know, you're talking about marriage and babies. It's enough to give a man heart failure. You're right. Forget I ever suggested the idea."

Norah hadn't explained herself well. She feared it sounded as though she was looking for a marriage proposal, and she wasn't. Refusing his job offer was simply a form of self-protection. Because it would be so easy to lose her heart to Rowdy Cassidy and she couldn't allow that to happen.

By his own admission, he wasn't the marrying kind, despite what he'd felt for Valerie. Nothing in Rowdy's life, not a wife, not children, would ever be more important to him than CHIPS.

ROWDY WAS DUE to be discharged from the hospital early the following morning. Norah had been on duty since 7:00 a.m.; at exactly nine, the flowers started arriving. Huge bouquets of roses and orchids, enough for every staff member on the second floor. Rowdy had ordered them to show his appreciation for the excellent care he'd received. The gesture touched Norah's heart, reminding her how thoughtful and generous he could be.

She'd braced herself for this day. Within a few hours, the infamous Rowdy Cassidy would be released from the hospital. He'd be out of Orchard Valley and out of her life.

Arrangements had been made for a limousine to pick him up at the hospital's side entrance, to avoid the ever-curious press.

Karen Johnson had asked Norah if she wanted to be the one to wheel him out, and she'd agreed. From the hospital the limousine would drive Rowdy into Portland, where he was scheduled to hold a short news conference before boarding a Lear jet for Texas.

His stay at Orchard Valley Hospital would soon be behind him. CHIPS and the world he knew best were waiting for him. Instinctively, Norah understood that once he left Orchard Valley he'd never return.

An hour later she was wheeling an empty chair down the corridor to his room when she saw her father. She was so surprised that she went stock-still.

"Dad, what are you doing here?"

"Can't a man come visiting without being drilled with questions?"

"Of course, but I didn't know any of your friends were here."

"They aren't. I've come to talk to that rascal Cassidy."

"Rowdy?"

"Got any other rascal cowboys I don't know about?"

"No...it's just that he's about to be discharged." She couldn't imagine what her father planned to say. In fact, the whole family seemed to be taking a new interest in Rowdy. Karen had mentioned that Colby had stopped in to see him the day before. Apparently the two men had hit it off and could be heard laughing. Rowdy hadn't mentioned the meeting to Norah, but then she hadn't had much of a chance to talk to him.

"Rowdy's driver will wait," her father said confidently. "I promise I won't keep him long."

"But, Dad..."

"Give us ten minutes, will you? And make sure we're not disturbed."

Norah's heart started to race. "You'd better tell me what you intend to say to him."

Her father abruptly stopped walking and placed a gentle hand on her shoulder. "I'm not going to say anything about my dream, if that's what's worrying you. It's likely to scare him so bad we'll never see hide nor hair of him again."

"Dad!"

"It wouldn't be a good idea, Norah. The minute he heard about those six youngsters, he'd be out of here so fast it'd make your head spin."

Rowdy, nothing. *Her* head was spinning a mile a minute. "Then why do you want to see him?"

"That, my darling Norah, is between me and the cowboy."

Norah possessed her mother's calm nature. She wasn't easily flustered, but her father had managed to do it in a matter of seconds. She paced outside Rowdy's door, wishing desperately that the walls weren't so thick and she could listen in on their conversation.

In less than the predicted ten minutes, which felt more like a lifetime, her father reappeared, grinning from ear to ear. Norah stopped cold when he sauntered out of the room.

"He's a decent fellow, isn't he?"

Norah was too numb to do anything more than nod. With a roguish wink, her father walked away.

It took her a moment to compose herself. When she hurried into Rowdy's room, he was sitting on the bed, fully dressed, his Stetson beside him.

"Your father was just here."

"I know," she said, doing her best to act casually. "Did he have anything important to say?"

Rowdy didn't answer right away, then he nodded. "Yeah, he did." But he didn't elaborate, and Norah was left with a long list of unanswered questions.

Robbins arrived to say the limousine was waiting. Norah brought in the wheelchair and adjusted Rowdy's leg in the most comfortable position. She took her time, until she realized she was only delaying the inevitable. Sooner or later she'd have to wheel him outside.

Mrs. Emerich was already sitting inside the limousine. The driver was waiting to assist Rowdy, and Robbins, too, seemed eager to do what he could. But

Rowdy dismissed their offers. "In a minute," he told them.

With the help of his crutches he maneuvered his way out of the wheelchair and stood upright. It was the first time Norah had seen him standing and she was amazed at what a large man he was. She came barely to his shoulders.

"Well, angel face," he said softly, his gaze holding hers, "this is goodbye."

She nodded, but found she couldn't speak for the lump in her throat.

"I wish I could say it's been fun."

Norah laughed. "You'll be your normal self again before you know it."

"I expect I will," he agreed. He reached out and very gently touched her face. "Take care, you hear?" Then he turned away.

CHAPTER SEVEN

ROWDY CASSIDY was a fool, Norah decided as he drove away without so much as a backward glance. The least he could have done was kiss her goodbye. The least he could have done was give her one last memory...

Norah straightened, more determined than ever to put the man out of her mind. And out of her heart.

She'd start immediately, she decided, marching back to the hospital with every intention of calling Ray Folsom, of the X-ray department. He'd asked her out to dinner a week or so earlier, but she'd been busy with Rowdy and had declined. Norah stopped at the receptionist's desk, planning to leave a message for Ray. Janice Wilson, who was on duty, glanced up expectantly when Norah approached.

"Anything I can do for you?" Janice asked.

Sighing, Norah placed both hands on the counter and opened her mouth to speak. Then she shook her head. She wasn't ready to date anyone.

Unless, of course, it was Rowdy Cassidy.

A week passed, and Norah swore it was the longest seven days of her life. Fortunately, the preparations for Steffie's wedding helped fill the void left by Rowdy's absence. There was some task to occupy almost

every evening and for that, at least, Norah was grateful.

She noticed how closely her family watched her, and
she did her best to seem cheerful and unconcerned. It
went without saying that Rowdy wouldn't call. He'd
laid his best offer on the table and she'd turned him
down. It was over; he'd made that clear.

"Have you heard from Rowdy?" Valerie asked
while the three of them sat around the kitchen table
assembling wedding favors. They filled plastic champagne glasses with foil-covered Belgian chocolates and
wrapped each one in pastel-colored netting, then tied
a silk apple blossom to the stem with pink ribbon.

"No," Norah said, resenting the question. She
struggled to keep the disappointment out of her voice.
"And I don't expect I will." It was on the tip of her
tongue to ask her sister the same question, but she
didn't. She assumed Valerie hadn't made a decision
yet.

"Knowing Rowdy, he's probably waiting for you to
get in touch with him," Valerie suggested.

"Me?" Norah asked, surprised by the suggestion
"Whatever for?"

"To tell him you've changed your mind and want to
come and work for him. I should know—it's the same
game he played with me."

Norah bristled. Her sister was baiting her, questioning her resolve, and that angered Norah. "He
knows better," she said stiffly, "and so do you!"

Valerie grinned, apparently pleased. "He's well-
known for his ability to play a waiting game."

"There's no point in trying that with me." Norah
twisted the netting around the plastic glass with un-

necessary vigor and handed it to Steffie, who attached the ribbon.

"Men don't seem to learn things like that as quickly as women," Steffie mused. "Rowdy Cassidy has a few things to figure out."

Norah didn't respond to her comment, and the discussion soon returned to more general topics.

The idea of calling Rowdy had never occurred to Norah. But suddenly it made sense that, as his nurse, she should inquire about his progress. Valerie had placed the idea in her mind, and now Norah began to consider it seriously.

"I wonder how Rowdy's doing," she said conversationally to her father that same evening. She would have thought he'd be the first to suggest she ask Rowdy about his recovery, but he hadn't.

"We would've heard something if he wasn't doing well, don't you think?" he answered grumpily. "The way those newspeople reported every little detail of his life, you can bet it'd be on national television if he suffered the least little setback."

So much for that. "Ray Folsom called this morning. I—I'm going to dinner with him tomorrow evening," she told her father. Dredging up some enthusiasm for the date was going to require an effort. But after a week of moping around the house, pretending she didn't miss Rowdy, Norah was determined to enjoy herself.

Ray had seemed surprised when Norah accepted the invitation. Despite her previous refusal, she'd decided, not entirely on impulse, to go out with him. He was exactly what she needed, she told herself. Even

Valerie approved when she learned that Norah was going out.

"It'll do you a world of good," Valerie assured her.

But when the time came for Ray to pick her up, Norah was no longer so sure of that. He brought her flowers and she found this thoughtfulness endearing but wished he hadn't. She instantly felt guilty; although she'd agreed to dinner with him, her mind was on Rowdy Cassidy, and that seemed unfair to Ray, who was gentle and considerate.

"Oh, Ray," she said, holding the small bouquet of pink carnations to her nose to breathe in their light scent. "How lovely."

He gave her a pleased smile. "I've been hoping we could get together, Norah."

She smiled back, biting her lip. Again she wondered if she'd made the right decision.

The phone rang while she was looking for a vase. Steffie caught it on the second ring and poked her head into the kitchen where Norah was busy chatting with Ray and arranging the flowers.

"It's for you. Do you want me to take a message?"

"Ah..." She glanced at Ray, who was leaning against the counter.

"Go ahead," Ray said, checking his watch. "We've got plenty of time."

Norah picked up the kitchen extension. "Hello," she said distractedly.

"Hello yourself, angel face."

Norah nearly slumped to her knees, she was so shocked. "Rowdy." She was grateful her back was to Ray. The color had drained from her face, and she felt weak and shaky.

"Have you missed me?"

"I—I've been busy."

"Me too, but that hasn't kept me from thinking about you."

Norah didn't dare admit he'd been on her mind from the moment he was discharged from the hospital. Not with Ray standing only a few feet from her. It wasn't in her to be so heartless.

"Listen, angel face," Rowdy continued when she said nothing. "I'm in Portland."

"You are?" Her heart pounded with glad excitement. He was less than sixty miles away.

"I'm working out some of the details on the expansion project with Robbins—I should be done in an hour or two. I was thinking I'd send a car for you now and by the time you arrive I'll be finished and we could have dinner."

"Oh, Rowdy."

"It'll be good to see you again. Damn it, I've missed you, and I'm hoping you feel the same way."

Norah felt like crying; Rowdy's timing couldn't have been worse. "I can't," she told him. "I'm sorry, but I can't."

"Why not?" he demanded impatiently. "Are you working?"

"I've already got other plans."

"Break them," he said with his usual confidence. "I probably won't be in the area again soon."

"I can't do that."

"Why the hell not?"

"I'm going to dinner with a friend and we're due to leave any minute."

A pause followed her announcement. "Male or female?"

"Male."

Norah could almost feel his anger vibrating through the wire. Rowdy seemed to think she should be willing to drop everything the moment he called her. He obviously assumed she'd spent the past week longing for him. True, she had, but she was determined to put those feelings behind her and to get on with her life. The man was impossible, she fumed. He must have known he was going to be in the area; it would have been a simple matter to arrange their meeting in advance. Instead he'd waited until the very last minute. As far as Norah was concerned, if he was angry at having his plans thwarted, he had no one to blame but himself.

She might have told him that if Ray hadn't been there.

"I see," Rowdy said after a long silence. "Enjoy yourself, then."

"I'm sure I will."

"Goodbye, Norah." Before she could say another word, the line was disconnected.

She closed her eyes, needing a moment to compose herself. When she turned around, she discovered Ray involved in conversation with Steffie. Her sister's eyes sought hers. "That was Rowdy," she said, hoping Steffie realized she would have appreciated some warning before she'd picked up the phone.

"I wasn't sure," Steffie admitted wryly, "but I thought it might have been. Next time I'll know."

"Are you ready?" Ray asked. He seemed unaware that anything was troubling her.

Norah nodded.

It surprised her how much she enjoyed her dinner
with Ray. He was genuinely charming and Norah
couldn't help responding to his carefree mood.

"You're in love with that cowboy, aren't you?" Ray
asked suddenly as he drove her home. When she didn't
respond immediately, he added, "I understand, you
know."

"I... don't know what I feel anymore," Norah admitted in a troubled voice.

"Love's like that sometimes," Ray said quietly. "I
like you, Norah, and I was hoping there'd be a chance
for us. But—" he shrugged and reached for her hand
"—everything will work out in the end," he said,
squeezing her fingers gently. "It generally does. If you
need proof of that, look at what's happened to your
sisters over the past few months."

Norah didn't know what to say. Ray was a wonderful man, considerate and gracious, and he'd make
some woman very happy one day. But not her.

Still holding her hand, he walked her to the porch.
He kissed her cheek, then whispered, "I wish it was me
you were so crazy about."

"I've been rotten company, haven't I?" Norah
asked guiltily.

He smiled, shaking his head. "Not at all. I just hope
that cowpoke realizes how lucky he is."

Norah sincerely doubted it. "Thank you for dinner, Ray. I had a wonderful time."

He kissed her once more on the cheek. "Good luck
with your cowboy."

She opened the door and waited while Ray walked
down the porch steps and got into his car. She waved

goodbye, staring down the driveway until he was out of sight before she stepped into the house.

Steffie was waiting in the entry. "Thank goodness you're back!" she burst out urgently.

"Is it Dad? Did he—"

"Rowdy Cassidy's here," her sister broke in, nodding toward the den.

"Here? Now?"

"Dad's kept him occupied," Steffie informed her, "but he's been here the better part of an hour and getting more restless by the minute."

Norah's heart was hammering wildly. She forced herself to calm down before walking into the den, even managing a smile.

Her eyes immediately went to Rowdy, who stood, leaning heavily on his crutches, gazing out the window that overlooked the front porch. It was obvious that he'd witnessed Ray's kiss. It was equally obvious that he wasn't pleased. He looked tall and lean and so damnably handsome that it was all Norah could do to stop herself from rushing into his arms.

"Rowdy," she said huskily. "This is...an unexpected surprise."

Her father got to his feet and winked at her. "I'll bring both of you a cup of coffee," he told them and conveniently exited the room, leaving Norah alone with Rowdy.

Using his crutches, Rowdy levered himself around to face her, his right leg thrust out in front of him. "I trust you had an enjoyable dinner," he said stiffly.

"Very," she returned, clasping her hands together.

"I'm glad to hear it." Although he sounded anything but glad. He was frowning as he studied her, and
Norah felt uncomfortable under his close scrutiny.

"Please sit down," she invited, gesturing toward the
chair. "I didn't know you planned to stop by."

"Would it have mattered?"

Norah winced at the undisguised anger she heard in
his voice. "I hope Dad kept you entertained," she
said, avoiding his question.

"He did." Rowdy sank into her father's chair and
Norah sat across from him, on the ottoman.

"Is there anything I can do for you?" she asked.

He nodded slowly. "You offered to give me the
name of a reputable agency," he said gruffly. "I'm still
in the market for a private nurse. I assumed I could do
without one. You seemed so sure I'd be just fine on my
own." The last words came as an accusation.

"And you're not?"

"No," he told her angrily. "I'm having one hell of
a time adjusting to these damn crutches."

"It'll get easier with practice. A nurse can't do that
for you, Rowdy. You'll have to learn to walk with
them yourself."

He muttered something she couldn't distinguish,
which was just as well, judging by the disgruntled look
he wore.

"I'll get the name and number of the agency for
you," she told him.

"Fine."

She left the room and discovered Steffie and her father standing just outside the door. They looked star-
tled, then glanced at her guiltily. Norah glared at them

both, knowing they'd blatantly listened in on her conversation with Rowdy.

Steffie cast her an apologetic smile, then hurried up the stairs; her father chuckled with wry amusement and wandered toward the kitchen, mumbling something about coffee.

Rowdy was massaging his right thigh when Norah returned with a slip of paper. "Your leg still aches?" she asked.

"It hurts like hell," he said in a blatant effort to gain her sympathy.

"Are you taking the medication as prescribed?" She handed him the paper.

"I forget," he answered brusquely. "That's another reason I need a good nurse."

"Nurse or nursemaid?" she inquired sweetly.

"Nurse," Rowdy muttered.

Norah knew exactly what Rowdy Cassidy was doing, and she wanted it understood right now that she refused to be manipulated. If he wanted something, he'd have to ask for it in plain English.

"You honestly think this agency will have what I need?" he asked, eyeing her closely.

"I'm sure of it."

"I prefer someone young," he said, then added, "and blond, if possible. Oh, and pretty."

Norah nearly laughed out loud. Since she hadn't immediately volunteered for the position, he was hoping to make her jealous. "You might be wiser to request someone competent, Rowdy."

For a long moment he said nothing. "It's been one week," he told her, his eyes steadily holding hers. "Seven days."

"It seems longer, doesn't it?" she asked softly, looking away, not wanting him to see how miserable and lonely she'd been and how hard she'd worked at pretending otherwise.

"Much longer," he admitted grudgingly. "Damn, but I didn't expect to miss you this much." He glared at her, and it took Norah a second to realize he was waiting for her to change her mind, to accept the position.

"I've missed you, too," Norah told him, weakening. He'd played on her sympathies and that hadn't worked. But her heart was vulnerable, and he knew it.

"Ever been to Texas this time of year?" he asked, clambering to his feet. Using the crutches with surprising deftness, he worked his way closer to her until mere inches separated them. Until there was only a single step between them. One small step, and she could walk directly into his arms.

Norah didn't know where she found the strength to stand still, to resist him.

"Have you?" he asked again.

Norah shook her head.

"It's the most beautiful place on earth."

"As beautiful as Orchard Valley?"

Rowdy chuckled. "You'll have to make that judgment for yourself." He was waiting. Waiting for her to come to him, to swallow her pride and sacrifice her own needs to his.

Norah knew exactly what would happen if she took that step, if she agreed to leave with Rowdy. She'd fall so deeply in love with him that she'd give up her own hopes and plans, her own pleasures—all the things that made her Norah. She'd be unable to refuse him anything. Already she was halfway there.

He'd made it perfectly clear that he had no intention of marrying. Nor was he interested in raising a family. Rowdy had admitted that even if Valerie had broken off her engagement to Colby, he wouldn't have married her.

And if he hadn't been willing to marry her sister, he wouldn't want her, either. For that matter, Norah wasn't sure she'd agree if he *did* propose. When she married, she wanted a husband, a man who'd be a constant part of her life, a man who shared her need for a settled existence, with a home and a family. Not a man like Rowdy...

Norah was too sensible and pragmatic not to recognize they'd face these issues sooner or later, even if he hadn't raised them now. And when it did happen, she wanted to be sure he knew where she stood. Because she'd be so head over heels in love with him that she couldn't think clearly.

"If the agency here isn't able to find you a nurse..."

"Yes?" he asked eagerly.

"I'm sure there are several in Texas with excellent reputations. I could ask around for you."

His face tightened. "Lord, you're stubborn."

"It runs in the family. I'm surprised you didn't butt heads with Valerie more often."

"I'm not," he muttered, moving awkwardly away from her. "We were both working toward the same goals. You and I are working at cross purposes." He limped toward the phone and called for his car. "You want something I'm not willing to give you."

"What's that?" she asked.

His eyes darkened. "You want my pride."

He was wrong, but no amount of arguing was going to convince him of that and Norah hadn't the strength to try.

"It was good seeing you again, Norah," he said unemotionally.

"You too, Rowdy."

"If you go out with Ralph again—"

"Ray," she corrected.

"Of course, Ray. I must have forgotten."

"There's no need to be sarcastic."

"You're right," he said in a tone so cool that it seemed to frost the air between them. "In any event, I wish you the very best. I'm sure the two of you have a lot in common."

Norah said nothing.

"I CAME the minute I heard." Valerie's concerned voice drifted into the kitchen from the front entry the following morning. "What did he say to her?" she demanded of Steffie.

"I'm not entirely sure. It seems he wanted her to reconsider and go to Texas with him as his nurse."

"Norah turned him down, didn't she?"

"She must have."

Her sisters appeared in the kitchen, both wearing compassionate expressions.

"I understand Rowdy stopped by last night," Valerie said gently, as though she considered Norah emotionally fragile.

"He was here, all right," she muttered, continuing to stir the batter for oatmeal-and-raisin muffins. Baking had always been a means of escape for her.

Some women shopped when they felt depressed; some read or slept or went to exercise classes. Norah baked.

"And?"

"And he left."

"Do you think he'll come here again?"

Clutching the bowl against her stomach, Norah whipped the batter vigorously. "Who knows?" But she hadn't expected to hear anything from him after his discharge; his visit had come as a complete surprise. However, Norah wasn't fool enough to believe it would happen again. Rejection was difficult for any man and harder for Rowdy than most, since he'd become so accustomed to getting his own way.

He'd come to her twice, and she'd turned down his offer both times. He wasn't likely to try again.

"Rowdy's been spoiled rotten," Valerie warned her.

"Isn't every man?" Norah returned calmly.

Valerie and Steffie exchanged a glance. "She'll be just fine," Steffie murmured and, smiling, Valerie agreed.

Norah wished she felt as confident.

Rowdy's name wasn't mentioned again until the following evening. Norah's father was watching the news when he excitedly called for her. "Come quick," he shouted.

Norah raced in from the kitchen to discover her father pointing toward the television. "Rowdy's on the local news."

She sank into a chair and braced herself for the sight of him. The Portland news anchor reported the expansion of the Texas-based software company CHIPS, which would soon be building in the area. He went on to comment that the final papers had been signed and that the owner of CHIPS, Rowdy Cassidy, was currently in town. The ground-breaking ceremony was due to take place in two weeks.

The camera switched from the anchor to a clip of Rowdy. Norah didn't focus on him, but on the statuesque blond woman in a nurse's uniform who stood behind him.

Her stomach felt as if someone had kicked her.

Young and blond, just the way he'd said. And pretty...

"Norah?" Her father's voice broke into her thoughts. "Are you all right?"

"Fine, Dad," she answered cheerfully. "Why shouldn't I be?"

The phone rang shortly afterward. Her father answered; apparently it was Valerie. Norah wandered back to the kitchen to finish preparing the evening meal. She went determinedly about the task, refusing to allow emotion to take control of her.

She'd made her decision.

Rowdy had made his.

"OH, STEFFIE," Norah said breathlessly, gazing at her sister. "You're so beautiful."

Steffie had chosen not to wear a traditional wedding gown, but a tea-length cream-colored lace dress with a dropped waist. A garland of fresh baby's breath and rosebuds was woven into her glossy dark hair.

Norah couldn't stop staring at the transformation she saw in her sister. Steffie looked not only beautiful but supremely happy; she glowed with serenity and a calm, sure joy.

"Everyone's outside and waiting," Valerie announced when she walked into the bedroom. She stopped abruptly when she saw Steffie.

"Oh, Steffie," she breathed, the tears welled in her eyes. "Mom would be so proud."

"I feel just as if she were here," Steffie whispered, reaching for her wedding bouquet. "I thought I was going to miss her so much today and the most amazing thing has happened. It's as if she's been standing right beside me. I don't think I've ever felt her presence more."

"I felt the same way the day Colby and I were married," Valerie confessed. "Her love is here," she added simply.

Norah had felt it, too, although she hadn't been able to put it into words.

"Dad's waiting," Valerie told them.

Emotion swirled through Norah. She was truly happy for her sister and Charles, but her heart ached. Never had she felt more alone, set apart from those she loved. Valerie had Colby and Steffie had Charles, but there was no one for her.

She walked down the stairs with her two older sisters and paused at the top of the porch steps.

White linen-covered tables dotted the sweeping expanse of the front lawn, its grass a cool, luscious green. White wrought-iron chairs were scattered about. A number of long tables groaned with an opulent display of food. The three-tiered wedding cake sat on a table of its own, protected by a small, flower-draped canopy.

The actual ceremony was to take place next to the apple orchard. The trees were heavy with fruit, and a warm summer breeze drifted through the rows, rustling the leaves. Soft music floated toward Norah and she realized the time had come for her to lead the small procession.

The side yard was filled with friends and family. Norah led the others down the center aisle to the flower-decked archway; Valerie followed and took her place beside her sister.

Steffie came next, escorted by their father. Every eye was on the bride, and Norah gazed proudly at her beautiful sister.

The loneliness she'd felt earlier unexpectedly left her. She sensed her mother's presence again, a sensation so strong that Norah was tempted to turn around, to see if Grace were actually there, perhaps standing behind her. The pain she'd experienced was replaced by a certainty that one day she, too, would discover the love her sisters had each found that summer.

Steffie paused before Pastor Wallen, who'd married Valerie and Colby a short five weeks earlier. She gently kissed her father's cheek and turned, smiling, to Charles.

Norah had never seen Charles look more dashing. She noticed the private smile he exchanged with his bride, the tenderness of his expression. Their love for each other was almost tangible.

Norah stood beside Valerie. Her own dress was the pink one she'd worn to Valerie's wedding. Val's was pale lavender. A sprig of baby's breath and silk apple blossoms was tucked at Norah's ear, and Valerie wore a pearl comb that had been their mother's. Steffie handed her bridal bouquet, of white rosebuds and pale silk apple blossoms, to Norah to hold during the ceremony.

Minutes later, Stephanie Bloomfield had pledged her love to Charles Tomaselli, and Pastor Wallen had pronounced them husband and wife.

A happy cheer rose from their guests, and Steffie and Charles fled laughing from a hail of birdseed.

Norah smiled after the happy couple, then frowned. An irregular, beating sound could be heard in the distance. She glanced about, wondering at its source.

It took her a few moments to realize a helicopter was approaching.

Everyone stopped and gaped in wonder as the aircraft slowly descended from the sky, landing on the driveway. Norah looked at her father, who moved forward.

Norah did, too, her heart pounding as hard and as loud as the whirling blades.

The door opened and two crutches appeared before Rowdy Cassidy levered himself out. He scanned the crowd until he found Norah. Then he grinned.

"I'm not interrupting anything, am I?" he asked.

CHAPTER EIGHT

"ARE YOU *interrupting* anything?" Norah repeated, laughing incredulously. "This is Steffie and Charles's wedding!"

Using the crutches, Rowdy swung his legs forward, then stopped abruptly. "*Another* wedding?"

Norah laughed again, so happy to see him that it didn't matter that they'd parted on such bad terms only a week earlier. She hurried to his side, threw her arms around his neck and hugged him.

She felt his sigh and knew he was no less delighted to be with her. The crowd started to disperse as the newlywed couple reappeared to lead the way across the lawn to the reception area.

"If I'd known there was a wedding taking place I would have avoided this place like the plague," Rowdy muttered.

"Why are you so set against marriage?" Norah asked, glancing up at him.

"Look what happened to me the last time I showed up for one of your family weddings." He moved his right leg forward for her to examine the cast, which reached halfway up his thigh.

"Good to see you again, Rowdy," Colby said, his arm tucked securely around Valerie's waist. The two men exchanged quick handshakes. David stepped forward to welcome him, too, chuckling about Rowdy's propensity for making grand entrances.

"When it comes to your daughters, I certainly seem to have a bad sense of timing," Rowdy told her father.

"Not in the least," David Bloomfield assured him, his gaze lighting on Norah. "In fact, it couldn't be better. Isn't that right, Norah?"

Laughing, she nodded, eager to agree. Not long before, she'd been feeling lonely and despairing; now Rowdy's dramatic arrival was like an unexpected gift.

The others drifted back to the wedding party, leaving Norah and Rowdy alone for the first time.

"How long can you stay?" Norah asked. It went without saying that their time together would be limited.

"A few hours. The ground-breaking ceremony for CHIPS Northwest is scheduled to take place later this afternoon."

Norah led him to a chair and helped him sit down. As he laid the crutches on the grass beside him, she glanced about. "Where is she?" she asked, referring to his blond nurse.

Rowdy didn't pretend not to know what she was talking about. He frowned and muttered something unpleasant under his breath.

"Pardon? I didn't quite hear that," she said sweetly.

"That's because it wasn't meant for you to hear. If I tell you, you'll gloat."

"No, I won't," she promised, doing her best to swallow a laugh.

"All right," Rowdy muttered, "since you insist on knowing. She didn't work out."

"And why's that? You were so sure you needed a nurse."

"I do... that is, I did need one. Unfortunately the nurse I hired was a daughter of Attila the Hun. The problem with you blondes is that you're deceptive-looking. You *look* like you'd be all sweetness and light."

"But we are."

Rowdy said nothing, but the grimace he sent her caused her to laugh outright.

"I still need a nurse," Rowdy argued, "but I only want you. Since you're being so blasted stubborn, I'm forced to make do on my own."

In a silent-film gesture, Norah pressed the back of her hand against her forehead and expelled a beleaguered sigh. "Life is tough, Rowdy."

He waved his index finger under her nose. "I knew you'd gloat."

"I'm sorry," she told him between giggles. "I really am, but I couldn't help myself."

Rowdy reached for her hands, gripping them in his own. "You're a sight for tired eyes, Norah. I've missed you more than—"

"What you miss is getting your own way," she interrupted tartly.

Rowdy grinned. "Tell me, have you gone out with Ralph lately?"

"It's Ray, and no, I haven't."

Rowdy hesitated. "I don't have the right to ask you not to date anyone else."

"No, you don't," Norah agreed.

"Nevertheless . . ." Rowdy's scowl deepened. "I don't mind admitting I was concerned about that guy."

"Why?" Anyone looking at her would know in an instant how deeply she cared for Rowdy. Ray was a friend, nothing more. She hadn't intended to make Rowdy jealous.

"I guess I'm more selfish than I realized," he said grudgingly. "I want you for myself."

Norah made a conscious effort to change the subject. There was no point in pursuing this; it was too painful and she knew nothing was going to change.

"Are you hungry?" she asked, noting that the guests were helping themselves to the large array of hors d'oeuvres and other dishes prepared by the caterers.

"Starved," Rowdy answered, but when she stood to get him a plate, he caught her hand. "It isn't food I need." His dark eyes held hers and Norah could feel herself moving toward him.

"Not here," she murmured, stopping herself.

"Where, then? Norah, I need to hold you so damn much. It's been driving me crazy from the moment I left the hospital."

"Rowdy, this is my sister's wedding."

"Surely you're allowed a few minutes alone."

"Yes, but . . ."

"Norah," he said decisively, "we need to talk."

"It isn't talking that interests you, Rowdy Cassidy, and we both know it."

"Ah, but what interests *you?*"

Norah sighed. "You already know," she admitted in a low voice.

Rowdy glanced around them, reached for the crutches and got to his feet. "Lead the way."

"Rowdy...I'm not sure about this."

"We'll pretend we're getting something to eat and before anyone notices we'll casually slip away. A few minutes, Norah, that's all I'm asking."

She hadn't the heart to refuse him—or herself. Their time together was so brief, and she needed him. She needed him more than she'd ever needed anyone, she thought.

If there were people who noticed how Norah and Rowdy eased themselves away from the festive crowd assembled on the front lawn, they didn't say. She steered Rowdy toward the side yard, near the orchard, where the ceremony had taken place. It was quiet and peaceful there. A light breeze wafted through the fruit trees.

Knowing it was more comfortable for Rowdy to sit rather than stand, she guided him to the first row of chairs in front of the archway.

"I certainly hope you're not hinting at something here," he muttered, nodding toward the tall flower-filled baskets. He carefully lowered himself into the chair, and Norah sat down next to him. Rowdy's arm settled over her shoulders. She rested her head on his chest and, sighing, closed her eyes.

She'd dreamed of moments like this. Moments of peace, without all the tension between them.

He stroked her hair and sighed, too. "I've never known a woman quite like you." His lips grazed her temple. "I've never known a woman who played checkers quite as poorly, either."

They both laughed, and Norah leaned her head back to look into his face. The laughter fled from his eyes. Instinctively, Norah moistened her lips in preparation for his kiss.

Rowdy didn't disappoint her. He lowered his mouth to hers in a kiss that was both gentle and undemanding.

Norah had never experienced anything sweeter. "Oh, Rowdy," she whispered with a soft moan of pleasure, her eyes closed. "I've missed you."

His mouth returned to hers, and this time, the kiss was long and hard. Norah was flooded with a need so powerful that she twisted around in her chair to entwine her arms around his neck. When they broke apart they were breathless.

"Come with me this afternoon," he pleaded.

The offer was so tempting that it was all Norah could do to refuse. "I want to, but I can't leave my family. Not on Steffie's wedding day."

Rowdy tensed and she realized he was dealing with his own disappointment. "I understand. I don't like it, but I understand."

"Tell me again," she whispered, glancing up at him, "how dreadful the blond nurse was."

"Were you jealous?"

"Insanely."

"Enough to change your mind?" he asked hopefully.

She shook her head. "I'm amazed at how well you've adapted to the crutches, though. You're doing splendidly without me."

His eyes grew serious. "That's where you're wrong, Norah." He kissed her again with an unleashed need that left her clinging and dizzy.

They wandered back to the wedding party a little later. Norah brought them both plates piled high with fresh fruit and a variety of hors d'oeuvres—bacon-wrapped scallops, tiny quiches, skewered shrimp. They fed each other tidbits, shared a glass of champagne and talked and laughed for what seemed like minutes but was in reality hours.

The helicopter arrived just after Steffie and Charles had cut the wedding cake. Norah watched the aircraft approach, feeling a sense of dread, knowing it would take Rowdy away from her.

She forced herself to smile. He'd been with her for several wonderful hours, the most uninterrupted time they'd had together in weeks.

Deep in her heart, she realized it would always be like this with Rowdy. A few minutes here, an hour there, squeezed in between appointments, stolen from schedules.

She stood alone on the lawn, the guests for the reception behind her, as the helicopter lifted toward the sky. She waved, her hand high above her head, until she was certain Rowdy couldn't see her any longer.

He hadn't told her when he'd see her again, but Norah knew it would be soon. It had to be. Neither of them could bear being apart like that again.

Valerie hurried to her side. "Are you going to be all right?"

Norah offered her sister a brave smile. "I'll be fine."

"You're sure?"

Eyes blurry with tears, she nodded.

Rowdy phoned her the next three nights, and they talked for nearly an hour each time. They spoke of nonsensical trifles, of daily details and of important things, too. She told him about Steffie and Charles's romance and why the newlyweds were honeymooning in Italy. Rowdy told her about his family, or rather lack of one—how his parents were killed when he was young and he'd been raised in a series of foster homes.

He always called late in the evening, and with the time difference it was well past midnight in Texas when they ended their conversations. He didn't need to tell Norah that he was missing an hour's sleep in order to talk to her. She knew it.

"I'm leaving for San Francisco first thing in the morning to meet with a group of important stock-holders," he told her on Tuesday night. "The meetings will probably run late. I doubt I'll get a chance to call you."

"I understand." And she truly did. CHIPS would always come first for Rowdy, because it was the family he'd never had, the security he'd grown up without. She understood his obsession with the business now, and the needs that drove him.

"It isn't what I want, Norah."

"I know." She wasn't angry, not in the least. "It's all right, Rowdy." She was trying to resign herself to the fact that it would always come to this. His company would remain the emotional center of his life. "When will you get home?"

"Saturday afternoon at the earliest."

"I'm working this weekend," she said, more because she needed to keep talking than because she felt he'd be interested in the information. "I had to trade with a friend of mine in order to have the weekend off for Steffie's wedding. We work on a rotating schedule at the hospital. It changes every four weeks so we can spend as much time with our families as possible."

"Why do you work?" He wasn't being facetious or sarcastic; his curiosity was genuine. It wasn't financially necessary for her to hold down a job, but she loved nursing and she *needed* to work, to occupy her time in a productive, responsible and fulfilling way. She expected Rowdy to empathize with those feelings.

"My mother was a nurse. Did you know that?"

"I must have, because it doesn't come as any surprise."

Norah smiled into the telephone receiver. "From the time I was a little girl, I knew I'd go into the medical profession."

"Did your mother work outside the home?"

"No, she quit soon after she and Dad married, when she was pregnant with Valerie."

"Did she miss the hospital?"

"I'm sure she did, but once we were a bit older she used her medical skills in other ways. When the migrant workers came to pick apples at our orchard and a couple of neighboring ones, Mom organized a health clinic for them—until she became too ill to do it any longer. Then she and Dad set up a fund, so the workers and their families could afford to go to the clinic at Orchard Valley." Norah swallowed hard. "She was a special woman, Rowdy. I wish you'd known her."

"I wish I had, too, but I already guessed she was someone unusual. She raised you, didn't she?"

That was about as romantic as Rowdy ever got with her. Norah didn't expect flowery words from him, certainly nothing more than a careless term of affection. Like "angel face"...

"It'd be a whole lot more convenient for us if you worked regular hours like everyone else," Rowdy said after a moment. "Some days you're on duty, some days you're not. Half the time you end up staying later than you're scheduled. I'm surprised you don't burn out with those long hours."

"Me work long hours?" she challenged with a short laugh. "Ha! You do the same thing. Even more so. It's a wonder *you* didn't burn out years ago."

"That's different."

"It is not," she insisted, "and we both know that. Only you're too proud to admit it." She paused thoughtfully. "Rowdy," she said, "I do agree that there's a difference. My life isn't dictated by my job the way yours is."

"What's so unusual about my dedication to CHIPS?" Rowdy countered sharply. "Don't forget I started the company. CHIPS is more than a job. No one's hiring me to work eighteen hours a day—I do it by choice."

Norah didn't need to be reminded of the truth of his words. With a small inward sigh, she changed the topic, asking questions instead about the San Francisco meetings.

When she'd finished the call with Rowdy, Norah wandered downstairs. Without consciously realizing where she'd been headed, she found herself standing in the doorway of her father's den.

"Would you like a cup of hot chocolate?" she asked. The offer was an excuse to talk, and she suspected her father would recognize it as such.

He did. Automatically setting aside his book, he glanced up at her. "Sure. Would you like some help?"

Before she had a chance to answer, he stood and followed her into the kitchen. While she took out the saucepan, her father retrieved the milk from the refrigerator. Norah was gratified to see how much more energetic he'd become lately; his recovery really had been nothing short of miraculous, she decided.

"How's Rowdy?" he asked almost as if he'd known exactly what she wanted to discuss.

"Good," she answered, hoping to appear nonchalant. "He's taking a business trip to San Francisco in the morning. I asked him how often he's been there, and he told me he's visited the Bay area a dozen or more times in the past half year."

"As I recall, Valerie took several trips there with him."

"I remember that," Norah said, "but did you know that in spite of all those times Rowdy's visited San Francisco, he's never been down to Fisherman's Wharf or walked through Chinatown or taken a cruise around the Bay. When I pressed him, he admitted he's never seen anything more than the airport and the inside of a hotel meeting room."

"Rowdy Cassidy's a busy man."

"Don't you understand?" Norah cried, surprised by the intensity of her emotion. "He's working himself to death, and for what? Some software company that will pass on to a distant relative he hasn't seen in twenty years. A relative who'll probably just sell his share of the stock. To strangers!''

"It bothers you that Rowdy doesn't have any heirs?'' her father asked as he brought down two earthenware mugs.

"What bothers me,'' she returned heatedly, "is that he's working himself to death for no real reason. He's a candidate for a heart attack—the same way you were. He's got atrocious eating habits, doesn't exercise and works too hard.''

David nodded and grinned. "You know what it sounds like to me?'' he asked, and not waiting for a reply added, "Rowdy Cassidy needs a wife. Don't you agree?''

AS HARD AS SHE TRIED to concentrate on her own duties, Norah couldn't keep her mind off Rowdy. He'd already told her he wouldn't be able to phone her, since his meetings with several important stockholders would last until all hours of the night. For reasons she didn't understand, Norah was restless all afternoon.

When she arrived home she found her father weeding the garden she'd planted earlier that summer. He straightened, grinning, and waved when he saw her.

"Looks like we've got enough lettuce here for a decent salad.''

Norah squatted down in the freshly weeded row and picked a handful of radishes. "We can add a few of these, as well.''

It was good to see her father soaking up the sunshine, looking healthy and relaxed. He was working part-time, managing the orchard, which kept him occupied without overtaxing him.

"Before I forget," her father said, "an envelope was delivered for you this afternoon. I think it's from Rowdy."

Norah didn't linger outside a moment longer. She couldn't imagine what Rowdy had sent her, but she wasn't waiting to find out. When they'd spoken the night before, he hadn't mentioned anything.

The envelope was propped against a vase of roses left over from Steffie's wedding. Norah's name was inked with a lavish hand across the front. Eagerly tearing it open, she discovered a first-class airline ticket to Houston.

Norah stared at it for a moment before she slowly replaced it in the envelope, which she set back on the end table. Apparently Rowdy had forgotten she was scheduled to work that weekend.

The phone rang, and when she answered it she heard Rowdy's voice. "Norah," he said, "I'm glad I caught you. Listen, I've only got a couple of minutes between meetings. I wanted to be sure the ticket was delivered. This is crazy. I'm supposed to be here negotiating an important deal, but all I can think about is how long it's going to be before I can see you again. Trust me, this is not the way to run a company."

"I can't fly to Houston this weekend, Rowdy," she said without preamble. "You already know that."

"Why not?"

"I'm working, remember?"

"Forgot." He swore under his breath. "Can't you get a replacement?"

"Not easily. Weekends are precious to us all, and even more so to those who are married and have families."

He didn't hesitate for an instant. "Tell whoever will work in your place that I'll pay them ten times what they normally make in a weekend. I need to see you, Norah."

"I won't do that."

She could feel his anger. "Why not?"

"I can talk until I'm blue in the face and you still won't understand. Just take my word for it, your plan won't work."

"You mean to say there isn't a single nurse in Orchard Valley who wouldn't leap at the chance to earn ten times her normal salary just for working your shift?"

Norah could see that nothing useful would result from her arguing. "That's what I'm saying."

"I don't believe it."

Norah sighed. "You're entitled to believe anything you wish, but I know the people I work with. It may come as a shock to you, but family is more important than money."

"Damn it," Rowdy said angrily. "Why do you make it so difficult?"

"Rowdy, I can't live my life to suit yours. I'm sorry, I really am, but I have a commitment to my job and to my peers. I can't rush off to Texas because you happen to want me there. Nor will I allow our relationship to become nothing more than a few hours snatched between meetings and at airports."

"You seem to be taking a good deal for granted," he said stiffly.

"How's that?"

"Who told you we had a relationship?"

Norah breathed in sharply at the pain his words inflicted. "Certainly not you," she answered calmly, belying the turmoil she felt. "You're right, of course," she said when he didn't respond. "I—I guess I'd put more stock in our friendship than you intended. I apologize, Rowdy, for taking our—*my*—feelings for granted—"

"Norah," he interrupted. "I didn't mean that."

She could hear a conversation going on behind Rowdy, but she couldn't make out the details.

"Norah, I've got to go. Everyone's waiting on me."

"I know...I'm sorry about this weekend, Rowdy, but it can't be helped. Please understand."

"I'm trying, Norah. Heaven help me, I'm trying. If I get a chance later, I'll give you a call."

"All right." She didn't want their conversation to end on a negative note, but knew it was impossible for him to talk longer.

"Rowdy," she called, her heart pounding. "I...love you."

Her words were met with the drone of a disconnected line. He hadn't heard her, and even if he had, would it have made any difference?

NORAH SHOWED UP for work Saturday morning, her thoughts bleak. She'd been reassigned to the emergency room, but her heart was in a plane somewhere over California on its way to Houston, Texas.

Refusing Rowdy's offer to spend the weekend with him, had been one of the most difficult things she'd ever done. And yet she'd had no choice.

Her relationship with Rowdy—and she *did* believe
they had a relationship, his harsh words to the con-
trary—had made it over several hurdles. They were
only beginning to understand and appreciate each
other. Despite the present and future problems, Norah felt a new and still shaky confidence, a sense of
optimism.

She hadn't heard from Rowdy, other than the one
harried phone call, since he'd left Texas. She remembered his saying that he'd be back in Houston sometime Saturday afternoon. Norah was scheduled to
leave the hospital at three and hoped to hear from
Rowdy shortly after she arrived home.

He hadn't said he'd phone, but she hoped—Norah
pulled herself up short. She was doing it already. Although she'd promised herself she'd never allow a man
to rule her life, she'd willingly surrendered her heart—
and her freedom—to Rowdy Cassidy. There wasn't a
single reason to hurry home, she reminded herself. If
Rowdy phoned while she was out, she'd return his call
later.

Satisfied that she'd put her thinking back on track,
she went about her duties. A little after eleven, the new
intern, Dr. Fullbright, came into the emergency room
to tell her she had a visitor in the waiting room.
Thinking it must be Valerie, who sometimes dropped
by to visit Colby, Norah thought nothing of the summons.

When she saw that it was Rowdy, she stopped cold.
He was exhausted, she noted. His eyes were sunken
and his features pale, but it didn't matter to Norah.
Never had she been more thrilled to see anyone.

"Rowdy?" she whispered, walking into his arms. One crutch fell to the floor as he held her against him. Norah drank in the sensation of solid warmth and felt an unexpected urge to weep. He was pushing himself too hard, putting in too many hours.

Repeatedly she'd refused his offer to become his private nurse, and for the first time she wondered if she'd made a mistake. Obviously he did need someone.

She knew from what Robbins had said that Rowdy hadn't hired a replacement for Valerie, convinced he'd be able to persuade her sister to return to CHIPS. Norah didn't know if that was still the case, but she assumed he was continuing to carry both loads himself.

"What are you doing here?" she asked.

"If you wouldn't come to me, I figured I'd have to come to you." His hand tangled in her hair as he spoke. "Have you had lunch yet?"

"No. I'll check and see if I can go now. We're not too busy, but I'll need to stay on the hospital grounds."

Rowdy nodded. "Can we go someplace private?"

If there was any such place in the hospital, Norah had yet to find it. "The cafeteria shouldn't be very crowded."

Rowdy didn't look wildly enthusiastic at her suggestion, but he agreed.

Norah led the way to the elevator, smiling at the two other nurses already inside, and regretted that she and Rowdy couldn't be alone. If they'd had at least the brief elevator ride to themselves, she might have found

the courage to repeat what she'd confessed at the end
of their last telephone conversation.

Norah was right; the cafeteria wasn't crowded and
they were afforded some privacy in the farthest corner. Once Rowdy was comfortably seated, his crutches
leaning against the wall, he caught her hand, effec-
tively preventing her from moving to the opposite side
of the table. "Sit beside me, Norah."

Something in his voice, in the way he was looking at
her, told Norah this wasn't an ordinary conversation.
When he'd asked for someplace private she'd assumed it was because he wanted to kiss her.

"Yes?" she asked, taking the seat.

Rowdy glanced around, apparently checking for
eavesdroppers. "All right," he said with a heavy sigh.
"You win."

"I win?" she repeated, frowning.

"I knew from the first what you wanted."

"You did?"

"It's what every woman wants. A gold ring on her
left hand. I told you earlier, and I meant it, I'm not the
marrying kind. I don't have time for a wife and a
family."

Norah was utterly confused, but she said nothing.

"I couldn't sleep last night," he muttered, "until I
figured out your game plan. Even when I had, it didn't
make any difference. I love you so damn much I can't
even think clearly anymore."

Norah remained bewildered, not knowing what to
think or say. She'd tried to tell him she loved him, but
he hadn't heard her in his rush to get back to his
meetings.

"I love you, too, Rowdy," she told him now, her voice soft.

His eyes gentled. "That helps. Not much, but . . . it helps."

Norah shook her head in confusion. "I'm afraid I've missed something here. What are you trying to say?"

His mouth dropped. "You mean you honestly don't know?"

Norah shook her head again.

"I'm asking you to marry me. I'm not happy about it, but as far as I can see it's the only way."

CHAPTER NINE

"YOU'RE NOT HAPPY about asking me to marry you," Norah echoed, too stunned to know what she was feeling.

"I told you before that I had no intention of ever marrying."

"Then what are you doing proposing to me?" she demanded. "Did you think I was so desperate for a husband I'd leap at your offer?" The numbness was gradually wearing away, and she was furious.

Norah had always been the Bloomfield with the cool head and the even temper. But her much-practiced calm was no match for this situation. Only a man like Rowdy Cassidy would have the nerve to insult a woman and propose marriage to her in the same breath.

"You're not desperate. It's just that—"

"That's not what I heard," she interrupted. "According to this oh-so-romantic proposal, you're declaring me the winner of some great prize, which I suppose is you. Well, I've got news for you, Rowdy Cassidy. I wasn't even aware I'd entered the contest!"

Rowdy clenched his jaw in an unmistakable effort to hold on to his own temper. "I don't believe that. You have me so tied up in knots, I don't know which way is which anymore. It wasn't enough that you turned down the job, but you had to torment me by dating other men!''

"One date! How was I supposed to know you'd want to see me the one and only night I'd made other arrangements? I'm not a mind reader, you know. Was I supposed to be so flattered, so—so *overwhelmed* by your summons that I'd cancel my evening with Ray?''

"Yes!'' he shouted.

"I refused to do that then, and I refuse to do it now. I *will not* spend my life waiting for an opening in your absolutely ridiculous schedule.''

Rowdy's hand sliced the air between them. "All right, fine. Let's just drop this thing with Ralph.''

"Ray!'' she shouted, attracting attention from those around her.

Both were silent for several embarrassed moments.

Finally, Rowdy exhaled sharply and said. "Shall we try this again?'' He studied her through half-closed eyes before proceeding. "I'll admit there were better ways of asking you to be my wife. The only excuse I have is thirty hours with no sleep.''

Norah mellowed somewhat. "Thirty hours?''

Rowdy nodded. "It didn't help that I was looking forward to your being there when I returned home. You might recall that you turned me down on that, as well.''

"It's not as though I didn't want to be with you,'' she assured him. "But you knew I was scheduled to work this weekend . . . I'd told you so myself, remember?''

"What's more important,'' he said through gritted teeth, "your job or me?''

"We keep rehashing the same thing," she said, throwing her hands in the air. "You want me to be at your beck and call. You're suggesting I should spend my life in limbo, waiting for you to find time for me."

"That's not what I mean at all," he said in a dangerously quiet voice. "But if you cared about me half as much as I care about you, you'd be willing to make a few minor adjustments."

"You want far more than *minor* adjustments. You want absolute control and I refuse to give you that."

"You're not even willing to compromise," he said bitterly. "With you, it's all or nothing." He looked away from her, glaring.

"Rowdy, I am willing to compromise. All I'm asking for is a little advance warning, so I know what to expect. Do you realize everything we've done has been on the spur of the moment? Nothing has ever been planned."

He nodded, a bit sheepishly. "That's not typical for me, you know. Falling in love with you has shot my concentration, not to mention my organizational abilities, all to hell."

"Oh, Rowdy." He could be so sweet and funny when he wanted. But he acted as if loving her was some kind of... weakness. He didn't see love as something that gave you strength, the way Norah did.

"Norah," he said, his voice softening. His hand reached for hers and his gaze was level with her own. "I love you. Will you do me the honor of becoming my wife?"

The tears that filled her eyes and her throat made speaking impossible. All because she loved him so much.... Norah blinked and realized there was no help for it. She grabbed a napkin from the shiny chrome dispenser in the middle of the table and blew her nose.

"I didn't have time to buy a ring," he told her, "but I figure you'd rather pick one out yourself. Go to any jeweler you want and have them send me the bill. Buy a nice big diamond—money's no problem. All I'm concerned about is making you happy."

Norah froze and closed her eyes at the unexpected stab of pain. Rowdy just didn't realize. No woman wanted to pick out her wedding ring alone, but she doubted Rowdy would understand that.

"I never meant to fall in love with you," she said softly, when she could speak.

"I didn't mean to fall for you, either," he admitted gruffly. "Hell, I didn't even know what love was. I liked Valerie and I missed her when she was here with you and Steffie during your father's surgery, but—" he shrugged "—love had nothing to do with it."

"What do you mean?"

"I thought I loved Valerie. I know how angry I got when I learned she was marrying Colby Winston. The fact is, I did everything I could to get her to change her mind. My ego took something of a beating, thanks to your sister."

Norah grinned at the memory. Rowdy wasn't accustomed to losing, and it had sorely injured his pride to have Valerie defy him.

"What I realized," he continued, "was that even if Valerie had broken off the engagement, I wouldn't have offered to marry her." Norah had already known that but made no comment. Rowdy sought out her gaze. "I was never in love with your sister. I might have thought I was at one time, but I know what love is now.''

''You do?''

Rowdy nodded. ''I'm not the marrying sort—fact is, I never thought I'd ever want a wife, but damn it all, Norah, you've got me so confused I'd be willing to do just about anything to make matters right between us. I'm offering you what I never would your sister or any other woman. If nothing else, that should tell you how serious I am.''

Tears ran unabashed down her cheeks.

''Say you'll marry me, Norah,'' he coaxed.

Norah reached for another napkin and dabbed at her cheeks. ''I . . . felt so lonely when Valerie and Steffie fell in love. It was as if the whole world had someone, but me.''

''Not anymore, Norah. We have each other.''

''Do we?'' she asked softly. Rowdy was making this so difficult. ''You'll have me, but who will I have? Who will be there for me?''

His eyes revealed how perplexed he was. ''I will, of course.''

''How can you possibly ask me to be your wife when you already have one?''

''That's ridiculous,'' Rowdy returned impatiently. ''I've never been married in my life. You're the only woman I've loved in more than thirty years. I don't know where you heard anything so outlandish, but it isn't true.''

''It isn't a woman I'm talking about, Rowdy, it's CHIPS.''

He shook his head and frowned at her. ''I don't understand.''

"You and I don't mean the same thing when we say love. To you CHIPS is everything. It's the one thing you really love—your family, your wife, your children. Your emotional security."

"You don't know what you're saying!"

"But I do! I've seen it happen over and over again. From the moment you were admitted to the hospital. Karen and I had to practically set up roadblocks in order to give you time to convalesce. Your corporate attorney was waiting outside the hospital door practically the instant he learned about your accident. You even had a phone installed with—I've forgotten how many lines. Remembering what a panic you went into the day word leaked out that you'd been involved in a plane crash?"

"I'm not likely to forget it. Stock in CHIPS dropped two points."

"You acted as if the world was coming to an end."

"You would, too, if you had a hundred million dollars at stake," he argued.

"Don't you understand?" she pleaded. "You don't have *time* in your life for anything or anyone else. Not me, not a family. No one."

Rowdy tensed. "What do you want from me, Norah? Blood?"

"In a manner of speaking, I guess I do. You can't go on the way you have been, working so many hours, not taking care of yourself. Eventually you'll collapse. As far as I can see, you're a prime candidate for a heart attack a few years down the road. I know you've got a management team, because Valerie was part of it, but you don't let them manage—you do it all yourself."

"I'm a candidate for a heart attack? Hell, you're just full of warmth and cheer, aren't you?"

"It's important that I explain my feelings. I don't mean to sound so pessimistic, but I'm worried about you."

"I wouldn't be too concerned if I were you," he muttered sarcastically. "I've got an excellent life insurance policy, and since you're so worried, I'll make sure you're listed as the beneficiary. Revise my will, too."

"Oh, Rowdy, for heaven's sake. I don't want your money, I want *you*."

He shrugged in apparent unconcern. "You wanted to be realistic? I'm only complying with your forecast of gloom and doom. And if I'm such a poor health risk, you'd best marry me now. The sooner the better, since my time's so limited."

"How can you joke about something like this?"

"You're the one who brought it up."

He was purposely misunderstanding everything she was trying to say. "What's important in life isn't things; it's people and relationships. It's the two of us building a life together, raising our family, making time for each other."

"Family," he repeated as if he'd never heard the word before. Sighing, he sagged against the back of the chair. "I should have known you'd want children. All right, we'll work around that. I'll agree to a child, but we stop with one, boy or girl. Agreed?"

Norah was too dumbstruck to respond.

Rowdy glanced at his watch, scowling. As usual, he was on a tight schedule, Norah thought wryly. He needed an answer and he needed it now. The luxury of his presence would always be limited, even to her.

Norah felt as though the whole world was crashing down around her. It was going to break her heart to refuse him, and what made it all the more painful was that she doubted Rowdy would ever really understand. He'd view her as irrational, demanding, sentimental.

"I've never wanted anything more in the world," she said, trying desperately to keep the emotion from her voice. She leaned toward him and pressed her hand to his face, then gently kissed his lips.

Rowdy seemed surprised by the small display of tenderness. "I'll make the arrangements with a jeweler," he said, preparing to leave. He reached for his crutches.

"Rowdy," she said quietly.

He must have heard a telltale inflection in her voice, because he turned back to her. She watched, amazed, as he read the look in her eyes.

The air between them went still and heavy. "You're turning me down, aren't you?"

She slowly exhaled, closing her eyes, and nodded.

Rowdy threw his Stetson down on the table in disgust. "Damn it all!" he shouted. "I should have known you were going to do this."

She sniffled and said, "Despite what you're thinking, this isn't easy for me."

"The hell it isn't." He stood and in his rush to leave, dropped one of his crutches, which frustrated him even more. Before he could prevent it, the second slammed to the floor and he slumped back down in the chair.

"I want a *husband*. It takes more than a few words said before a preacher to make a marriage."

"But you aren't going to marry me, so there's no need to belabor the point, is there?" He managed to pick up one crutch, and with it was able to retrieve the second. He obviously wanted to get away from her as quickly as possible, moving awkwardly through the cafeteria. She followed close behind.

"You got what you wanted—what you were after in the first place. You worked everything out well in advance, didn't you?"

"Worked out what?" A sick feeling attacked Norah's stomach.

He paused to look at her, his expression cynically admiring. "I have to hand it to you, Norah Bloomfield, you're quite the actress. Am I right in guessing that you worked all this out beforehand so I'd make a fool of myself proposing and you'd have the pleasure of turning me down?"

"Rowdy, that isn't true." Shocked, she trailed him out of the cafeteria. "It's just that I'd never be content with the leftover pieces of your life, with a few minutes shaved here and there."

"Then it's best to know that now, isn't it?"

"Yes, but—"

"You're fighting a losing battle, sweetheart. I suggest you drop it. CHIPS made me what I am today, and I'm not about to give up my company so you can lead me around by a ring through the nose." He forcefully jammed his thumb against the button to summon the elevator.

"I don't want you to give up CHIPS," she protested, but he cut her off.

"Why is it we're discussing all *your* wants? Frankly, they're overwhelming." He held himself stiffly away from her, leaning heavily on his crutches and staring at the floor numbers above the door.

When the elevator arrived, Norah stepped back and allowed Rowdy to enter. With some difficulty he did so, then turned around to face her. If he was surprised she hadn't followed him inside, he didn't reveal it.

"Goodbye, Rowdy."

"It *is* goodbye, Norah. Don't worry about me. I plan on having a damn good life without you."

The elevator doors glided shut, and she slowly pressed her hand over her mouth to hold in a cry of pain. Deliberately, she removed her hand, as if she were throwing him a farewell kiss.

"How is she?"

Valerie's voice drifted through the cubicle door. Norah could have answered for herself. She'd been emotionally devastated, but she was much better now.

Although Norah had returned to the emergency room, she wasn't in any condition to work. Not knowing what to do, her supervisor had called Colby, who was on duty.

Colby had tried to listen, but hadn't been able to understand her, she was crying so hard. Her incoherent attempts to explain had merely frustrated him. Apparently he'd phoned Valerie, and she'd rushed to the hospital.

"She should go home, but I don't think she's in any shape to drive," Norah heard Dr. Adamson tell her sister.

Everyone was making it seem far worse than it was, Norah thought grumpily. Okay, so she was a bit weepy when she returned from lunch. And it was true that she hadn't been able to speak too clearly, which made her cry even more with frustration. But everything was under control now—well, almost everything.

"Norah?" Valerie knocked softly on the door of the emergency-room cubicle, before letting herself in.

"Hi," Norah said, raising her right hand limply. "I'm doing much better than Dr. Adamson would have you believe."

"Colby's the one who's so concerned. He's never seen you like this."

"I don't think I have, either," she said, making an effort to smile. A pile of crumpled tissues lay on the gurney beside her. "I'm sorry everyone was worried about me, but really I'm fine. Or at least I will be in a little while."

"Do you want to tell me what happened?"

Norah shrugged and reached for a fresh tissue, clenching it tightly in her fist. "There's not that much to tell. Rowdy dropped in unexpectedly and asked me to marry him. I . . . didn't feel I had any option but to refuse."

Valerie looked as if she suddenly needed to sit down. "Let me see if I understand you correctly. Rowdy— Rowdy *Cassidy*—actually proposed?"

Norah nodded.

"He asked you to *marry* him?" Valerie asked incredulously.

Again Norah nodded. "I don't know why—he doesn't have time for me in his life. He . . . he wanted me to pick out my own engagement ring."

"I don't understand," Valerie said, frowning. "I thought you were in love with him."

"I am, and I'm sure he loves me—as much as Rowdy's capable of loving anyone."

It was as though Valerie hadn't heard her as she started pacing the tiny cubicle. "Every single person who saw you and Rowdy at Steffie's wedding was convinced your engagement would be next."

"He's already married—to CHIPS," Norah whispered sadly.

"So?"

"Don't *you* understand?" Norah cried, disappointed in her sister. She'd expected sympathy from Valerie, not censure.

"I guess I don't," Valerie admitted reluctantly. "What do you expect him to do—resign from the company, give up everything he's worked so hard to achieve all these years?"

"No...of course not." Norah felt shaken. All along she'd assumed she was right, but Valerie was forcing her to question her own actions.

"Now isn't the time to worry about it," Valerie said soothingly. "Dr. Adamson asked me to drive you home. You're much too upset to work."

"But what if—"

"Don't worry, Colby said he'd cover for you."

Norah didn't even get a chance to finish. She'd started to say *What if Rowdy calls and I'm not here?* But he wouldn't phone. Norah would have staked her career on it. He was much too angry—he'd told her their goodbye was final.

SOMEONE MUST HAVE called her father, because David was standing at the front door waiting when Valerie pulled into the driveway in front of the house. He poured Norah a stiff drink, told her to sip it slowly and then advised her to nap.

Norah did so without argument. She must have been more exhausted than she realized; she didn't awaken until late the following morning.

Valerie was speaking to her father when Norah walked down the back staircase into the kitchen. They abruptly stopped talking when she appeared. It didn't take a genius to figure out what they were discussing.

"Well," Norah said casually, "what did you two decide?"

"About what?" her father questioned.

"Me. And Rowdy."

"There isn't anything for me to decide," David said, exchanging a knowing smile with Valerie. "You've got a good head on your shoulders. You know what's best for yourself."

Norah wished she shared her father's confidence. Rejecting Rowdy's marriage proposal was the right thing to do—wasn't it? Good grief, he didn't even have half an hour to look for an engagement ring with her! Their marriage would be a continual battle of wills. She could fight another woman for his affections, but she was defenseless against a company he'd built from the ground up, a company that was his whole life. She had no choice but to make a stand now or be miserable later.

TEN DAYS PASSED, and Norah lived with a constant sense of expectation. But she wasn't sure what she was waiting for. Rowdy had made it plain that she wouldn't be hearing from him again.

Her father, too, seemed smitten with a feeling of hopefulness. More times than she could count, Norah saw him sitting on the porch, his gaze focused in the distance as if he was waiting for someone to come barreling down the long driveway.

"He isn't coming, Dad," Norah said one evening after dinner. She brought him a cup of coffee and sat down on the front step near him.

"You're not talking about Rowdy, are you?"

"Yes, Dad, that's exactly who I'm talking about."

"I don't expect he'll come. He's got too much pride for that. Can't say as I blame him. Poor fellow's head over heels in love, and by heaven, he doesn't know what to do about it. I feel sorry for the poor chap."

"He was furious with me. He might have loved me at one point, but he doesn't now." She was certain that Rowdy had completely blotted her from his mind.

"Isn't he scheduled to be out of his cast soon?"

Norah had to stop and think. She tasted the coffee, hoping its warmth would chase away the chill she felt whenever she thought about Rowdy. Her life felt so lonely, so cold without him.

"If I remember right, he should have had the cast removed on Monday." She didn't envy his physical therapist. Rowdy Cassidy was going to be a cantankerous and difficult patient.

As they were talking, Norah noticed a thin trail of dust rising from the driveway. Her father saw it, too, and Norah watched him relax, as though a long-awaited visitor had finally arrived. But Norah didn't recognize the car—or the driver.

Not until Earl Robbins climbed out of the car did Norah remember who he was. Rowdy's employee. The one who was heading up CHIPS Northwest.

"Hello again, Norah," he greeted her, closing his door and walking toward the porch.

"Hello," she said, trying to disguise her puzzlement. She introduced her father, and as she did so, tried to imagine what had brought Robbins to see her. A sense of panic filled her when she realized something must be wrong with Rowdy.

"Is Rowdy all right?" she asked, hoping he didn't hear the near-hysteria in her voice. "I mean, he's not ill, is he?"

Robbins glanced toward David and shook his head. "I'm here because of Rowdy, but I don't want you to worry. To the best of my knowledge, he's in fine health."

"Take the young man into my den," her father instructed. "I'll see about getting some iced tea, unless you'd prefer coffee or something stronger."

"Iced tea would be fine," Robbins said with a grateful smile.

Norah directed him into her father's den and closed the door, leaning against it with her hands behind her as she tried to compose herself.

"Valerie suggested I come and talk to you," he explained, pacing as he spoke. "To be honest, I'm not sure I'm doing the right thing. I do know that Rowdy wouldn't approve of my being here. He'd have my job if he knew I was within fifty miles of this place."

If Earl Robbins didn't feel the need to sit down, Norah did. She sank onto the ottoman and clenched her hands together in her lap. "How is he?" she asked, hungry for news of him.

Robbins ceased pacing. "Physically I'd say he's on the mend. The cast is off, and he's walking with the help of a cane. He's more mobile than he was, which helps—but not much."

"You didn't come here to tell me how well his leg is mending, did you?"

Robbins grinned wryly. "No, I didn't." He walked over to her father's desk and turned around to face her. "It isn't any of my business what went on between you and Rowdy. In fact, I'd rather not know.

"I realize he's in love with you. Both Kincade and I saw it happening. We sort of enjoyed watching the transformation. I'm no expert when it comes to love. Hell, I'm not married myself. But it seemed to me that you felt just as strongly about Rowdy."

"I do," Norah admitted. "Oh, I do."

"From the minute Rowdy was discharged from the hospital, all he did was think about you. He drove the staff crazy. It's a miracle that group of stockholders didn't walk out on him in San Francisco. Mrs. Emerich told me he bolted upright in the middle of the conference, as if he didn't know where he was, then he sat down and mumbled something no one heard."

"He was probably worried about what was happening to his stock," Norah said.

"I don't think so. My guess, and that of everyone else who's close to him, is that it was you he was thinking about in San Francisco. The same way he has ever since you two met."

"He isn't thinking about me any longer," Norah said, swallowing the hurt.

"Don't kid yourself. I'm not here for my health, Norah, and if Rowdy ever found out, he'd have my hide, as well as my job. He's miserable."

"I suppose he's making everyone else miserable, too."

"No, and that's what's got us worried. I've never known Rowdy to be so...nice. He's keeping his unhappiness to himself. He's polite, cordial, thoughtful. No one knows what to make of it."

"I—I'm sure it'll pass."

"Perhaps," Robbins agreed, "but I can't help thinking it might not. No one's ever seen Rowdy like this. We don't know what to do to help him. You've got your family, but Rowdy doesn't have anyone."

"He's got CHIPS," she said stiffly, not meeting the man's direct gaze.

A knock sounded on the door then, and her father brought a glass of iced tea to Robbins. He glanced from him to Norah and back again, then edged out the door.

"Thank you." Robbins took a sip of tea and set the glass aside. "I came because Valerie seemed to think it was important for you to know what was happening to Rowdy. She wants you to understand how very much he misses you...how lonely and lost he is. That's all. Now I won't take up any more of your time."

"Thank you for telling me." Although Norah knew Valerie had encouraged him to come, she remained grateful. Earl Robbins had given her a lot to think about.

He nodded. "Listen, if it wouldn't be too much to ask, I'd appreciate if you didn't say anything to Rowdy about my stopping in."

"Of course," Norah agreed.

Robbins looked significantly relieved.

It took Norah only about two minutes to decide what she needed to do with the information Robbins had given her, and two days to make the arrangements.

She kissed her father on the cheek late Thursday afternoon, picked up her suitcase and headed down the porch steps to Valerie's car. Her sister was waiting to drive her to the airport.

"You call, you hear?" her father shouted after her.

"Of course I will," Norah promised. "Although he just might throw me out on my ear."

David chuckled. "That isn't likely. That man needs you—the same way I needed your mother. Be gentle with him. The poor devil doesn't have a clue what's about to happen."

Norah found his parting words a bit odd. She didn't have a clue herself as to what was going to happen. All she could do was hope for the best.

Early Friday morning, Norah arrived at CHIPS dressed in her best suit. The seventeen-floor headquarters was an amazing piece of architecture, designed in smoky black glass and glistening steel.

The first thing she realized was how far from Orchard Valley she'd come, but that didn't deter her from her purpose. Armed with Valerie's directions and an elevator code, Norah entered the top floor that housed Rowdy's office.

"Ms. Bloomfield," Rowdy's secretary said softly when she saw Norah. The middle-aged woman slowly stood up and beamed her a wide smile.

"Hello, Mrs. Emerich," Norah said uncertainly. She was having a difficult time taking everything in. She'd had no idea CHIPS was so big.

"Oh, my heavens, I'm so glad you're here." Rowdy's secretary hurried from behind the desk and hugged Norah enthusiastically. "It was what we've all been praying would happen—your coming, that is. Rowdy isn't in the office just yet...I never know when he's going to show up these days. Would you like to wait for him?"

Norah nodded and followed Mrs. Emerich into Rowdy's private office.

"I'll get you some coffee," the older woman said, hands fluttering in her eagerness. "Sit down, anywhere you like. Just make yourself right at home." She turned to leave. "Oh, Norah, I'm so glad you've come..."

Perhaps it was a bit presumptuous of her, but Norah chose Rowdy's chair. She sat in the plush black leather and whirled around to face the window, with its dramatic view of Houston.

Hearing someone step inside the room, she turned around and smiled, expecting to see the secretary. Only it wasn't Mrs. Emerich who'd entered the room, it was Rowdy Cassidy himself. And he didn't look pleased.

"Just what the hell do you think you're doing in my office?" he demanded.

CHAPTER TEN

"ROWDY." Norah couldn't take her eyes off him. It was the first time she'd seen him stand without his crutches. He looked tall and proud—and unyielding. It didn't matter; Norah had never loved him more than she did at that moment.

"What are you doing here?" he demanded a second time.

"I—I came to talk. Sit down, please."

He leveled the full force of his scowl at her. "You're in my chair."

"Oh . . . sorry." She leaped up as though propelled by a spring and hurried around to the other side of the desk.

"Unfortunately, you made an error in assuming I wished to speak to you," he informed her coldly once he was seated. "As it happens, I have several appointments this morning."

Just then Mrs. Emerich appeared, carrying two steaming coffee mugs, which she set down on the desk. "Good morning, Mr. Cassidy," she said cheerfully. Winking at Norah, she continued, "Mr. Deavon called and canceled his nine o'clock appointment."

Rowdy glared at her as if he didn't believe her. "Call Kincade and have him here by nine."

"I'm sorry, sir, but Mr. Kincade phoned in sick."

"Murphy, then!"

"Mr. Murphy's out, as well," she informed him, then glanced at Norah and winked again. With that, she was out the door, closing it quietly behind her.

"Damn fool woman," Rowdy muttered. "All right," he growled, "you wanted to talk. So talk." He looked at his wristwatch. "I'll give you exactly five minutes."

Norah made herself comfortable in the leather chair across from him and deposited her large purse in her lap. The zipper made a hissing sound as she opened it. She rummaged through, then gave up and leaned forward to sip her coffee, noticing that Rowdy hadn't touched his.

"I thought you wanted to talk," Rowdy reminded her impatiently.

"I do, but I brought a list with me and I want to go over it with you."

"A list?"

She nodded absently, sorting through a variety of objects in her purse. "There are several important issues I feel we have to discuss." She still couldn't seem to locate what she needed and ended up setting her billfold and a paperback novel on the edge of his desk. She could feel Rowdy's disapproval, but was determined not to let him distract her. "Here it is," she said triumphantly, taking the folded slip of paper from the bottom of her oversized bag.

After returning everything to her purse, she zipped it shut. "Now," she began in a businesslike voice, "the first thing has to do with the engagement ring."

Rowdy's face tightened. "You can skip that one."

"Why?" She looked up from her list.

"Because there won't be one."

"All right," she said with a meaningful sigh. "I'll go on to item number two. The vice president. You've got an excellent management team, but as I said earlier, you take on far more than necessary yourself, so I'm suggesting you appoint a vice president you could work closely with over the next few years."

"Vice president of what?"

"CHIPS," she returned shortly. "What else? The way I figure it, you're going to need two, and possibly three. Valerie said she'd recommend Bill Somerset, John Murphy and/or Earl Robbins. All three are familiar with the operation of CHIPS and excellent managers. Valerie also seemed to think it would be a good move because you're probably going to lose Somerset if you don't promote him."

"In a pig's eye," Rowdy argued. "Bill's completely happy working for me."

"Perhaps now, but he'll be wooed away by some other company that'll trust him with added responsibilities. A vice presidency is a natural progression for him."

"What makes you so confident of all this?"

"I'm not," she readily admitted, "but Valerie obviously knows a lot more about it than I do. These are her recommendations."

"I gathered as much."

She moved her fingernail down the list. "Another thing. We'll need to make some kind of compromise on the issue of traveling."

"Traveling?" he repeated.

"I'm not sure how much is justified or necessary, but I'd appreciate having it held down to a minimum.

I imagine I'll be able to go with you on some trips. It would be ideal if we could combine business with pleasure. Maybe two or three times a year—depending, of course, on our schedules.''

Rowdy's response was a humorless laugh. "You must be joking. I take that many trips in a month."

"Exactly. That's far too much. The children won't even know they have a father if you're gone that often."

"Children?" he exploded.

"That's point number seven, but since you mention it, I'll address the subject now. I'd like more than one child. I enjoy children, Rowdy, and I'm looking forward to being a mother. Now, I agree that six may be out of line, but—"

"Six." He leaned forward, arms rigid and hands clutching the edge of his desk.

"I know, I know," she said with a sigh. "My dad seems to have that number fixed in his mind. But don't worry, I was thinking four would be quite adequate. It'd be nice if we had two boys and two girls, but it really doesn't matter."

Rowdy eyed her as if she'd gone completely berserk.

"Item number three," Norah went on without a pause. "You probably won't ever work less than forty hours a week and more likely it'll be fifty. Valerie told me there were times you didn't even bother to go home—you just slept at the office. However, I feel that would be detrimental to your health and to our relationship. If I'm going to marry you and move to Houston, I'd appreciate if you made an effort to come home every night. I do realize you're needed here and

I can live with whatever hours you deem necessary, provided the house is within easy commuting distance.''

''Anything else?''

''Oh, yes, there are several smaller items. Things any couple needs to go over before marriage.''

Rowdy made a show of glancing at his watch. ''You might want to hurry since you've got approximately two minutes left.''

''Only two minutes?''

He nodded, his look stern and unwavering.

''All right,'' she said, folding the slip of paper in her hand. ''I won't waste any more of your time with compromises.''

''Fine.''

''I'll talk about the most important reason for my coming here. I made a mistake when I rejected your marriage proposal, Rowdy. You caught me off guard—I wasn't expecting it. You were right, all I could think of was what I wanted, not what you were looking for in our relationship. So I've given you my list of possible compromises to think over.''

''One minute left.''

Norah stood, forgetting that her purse was in her lap. It fell unceremoniously to the floor. She stooped down to pick it up and straightened awkwardly. ''Could we meet and talk again soon? Then I'll listen to whatever you have to say. Actually, I'd be interested in knowing why you want to marry me when you've always been so dead set against marriage.''

''Which is the question I've been asking myself for the past two weeks. It's unfortunate that you don't understand business practices, Norah.''

"I don't even pretend to."

"And that explains your coming. You see, the offer was made and you rejected it."

"Yes, but as I told you, I acted in haste. I should have thought things through before I—"

"Apparently you don't understand," he said without emotion. "I've withdrawn my offer."

She blinked, and a feeling of dread attacked her heart. "But—"

"It's too late, Norah. Two weeks too late."

A numbness took hold of her limbs and she forced herself to exhale slowly. "I see... I'm sorry. I assumed, erroneously it seems, that your proposal was genuine."

"At the time it was."

"No, Rowdy, it couldn't have been. Love isn't a business transaction, something to be offered and retracted at will. It's a *feeling* and it's a commitment. That doesn't disappear overnight."

"I'm not an impulsive man, Norah...generally," he added with some reluctance. "But I was when I proposed to you. Actually you did us both a favor by rejecting my offer."

Norah was too stunned to respond for a moment. "You don't mean that?"

Rowdy said nothing, and since there didn't seem to be anything more for her to say either, she turned away from him, barely aware of where she was going.

"Goodbye, Norah."

She didn't answer him and walked blindly out of his office. She paused and closed her eyes for a moment to compose herself before proceeding.

Mrs. Emerich's voice drifted toward her. "My, that didn't take long, did it?"

"Not at all," Norah returned cordially, smiling at the older woman. She stood, as though paralyzed, in the outer office. She'd made such a fool of herself coming to Rowdy like this!

"Are you all right?"

It took a moment for the secretary's question to sink into her consciousness. "Ah...oh, yes, I'm fine. Thank you for asking." She glanced toward the closed door that led to Rowdy's office. "Take care of him for me, will you, Mrs. Emerich? He doesn't eat right and he works far too many hours. He—he needs someone."

"I've been telling him that myself for the past five years, but he doesn't listen."

"He's too stubborn for his own good," Norah agreed with a weak smile.

"Won't *you* be here? I was so hoping you two could patch up your differences."

Norah slowly, sadly, shook her head. "I'm afraid I...waited too long."

Mrs. Emerich's eyes revealed her dismay. "Oh dear, and I was sure everything would work out between you."

"So was I," Norah whispered and headed toward the elevator.

THE HOTEL where she was booked was a short distance from CHIPS's headquarters. Norah almost wished she'd walked, but with traffic so heavy and huge semitrucks roaring up and down the streets it didn't seem prudent, so she opted for a taxi.

The first person she called when she arrived back at the hotel was Valerie. When she told her sister what had happened, Valerie exploded.

"The man's a fool!" her oldest sister insisted. "He's pulling the same thing with you that he tried with me. Obviously he didn't learn anything the first time. Fine, we'll just have to teach him all over again."

"He didn't try to bribe me, Valerie, nor did he issue any threats."

"How could he? You're holding all the cards."

Norah didn't understand her sister, and frankly she felt so defeated and miserable that it didn't matter. "I've already changed my flight plans. I'll be home this afternoon."

"No, you won't," Valerie told her forcefully. "That's exactly what Rowdy expects you to do. He doesn't mean a word of it, you know."

"That's not the impression he gave me."

"Wait and see," Valerie assured her. "My advice to you is stay exactly where you are. Take in the sights, do a little shopping, relax, vacation. The last place Rowdy will ever think of looking for you is in his own backyard."

"But, Valerie—"

"Promise me," Valerie demanded. "Not a peep out of you. I can't get over this," she fumed. "That man's certainly a slow learner! Don't you worry, though, we're going to educate him once and for all."

"He isn't going to call me."

"I'm betting you'll hear from him in twenty-four hours. Thirty, tops."

"All right," Norah agreed reluctantly, although from the look on his face, Norah couldn't imagine hearing from Rowdy in thirty *days,* let alone thirty hours.

"Trust me, Norah. I know how Rowdy Cassidy operates. The only way he can deal with emotions is by treating everything like a tricky negotiation. A business deal."

"I did what we discussed. I approached him as though it was a business deal, and I went through my list."

"Good. That he can understand."

"But it didn't do any good."

"It will, it will. Now stay right where you are, and I'll let you know as soon as we hear from the great and mighty Rowdy Cassidy."

Norah wasn't sure she was up to playing hide and seek, but she trusted her sister and readily accepted Valerie's advice. Really, she had no other option if she intended to work out her relationship with Rowdy.

For two days she lazed around the hotel pool in the morning, shopped in the afternoon, and visited museums and art galleries. In the evenings she dressed for dinner and dined alone at the hotel. She'd never felt lonelier.

On the morning of the third day, her phone rang. Norah was still in bed, although it was almost noon. She'd stayed awake most of the night worrying, certain that she should have arranged a flight back to Orchard Valley. Hanging around a hotel room like this was crazy.

"He's here," Valerie whispered when Norah answered the phone. "Dad's talking to him now, and he's doing a masterful job of keeping a straight face. He's pretending he doesn't know where you are."

Norah scrambled into an upright position. "You mean Rowdy's there...in Orchard Valley...right this minute?"

"Exactly. None too happy, either, by the looks of him."

"Aren't you going to tell him I'm in Houston?"

"I might. Then again I might not."

"Valerie Winston, that's cruel. Put Rowdy on the phone right now. I insist. Do you hear me?"

"I'll make it up to him," Valerie promised with a delighted chuckle. "Colby and I've talked it over and I've decided to accept Rowdy's offer to head up CHIPS Northwest. Hold on a minute, and I'll get him for you."

A minute had never lasted longer. Although she strained to hear what was happening in the background, Norah could only catch bits and pieces of the conversation. The next instant Rowdy was on the line.

"Norah?"

"Hello, Rowdy. I—"

"Valerie says you're in Houston. Is that true?"

"Yes."

He cursed under his breath. "No doubt Valerie put you up to this. If I wasn't so grateful she's agreed to take on the Northwest assignment, I'd have her hide for this." Norah could hear her sister saying something in the background and Rowdy saying something in return.

"Listen, I'm on my way back to Houston. Will you meet me at the airport?"

"Of course. I love you, Rowdy. I kept thinking of all the things I should have said to you and didn't. It wasn't until I got back to the hotel that I realized I hadn't said the most important thing of all, and that was how much I love you."

"I love you, too. You are going to marry me, aren't you?"

"Oh, yes."

"Bring your list with you. There're a couple of points we need to discuss. Oh, before I forget, Bill Somerset's my new vice president."

"Oh, Rowdy, I do love you!"

"You know," he said with a heavy sigh, "I could get used to hearing you say that. Fact is, I could even get accustomed to being a husband—and father."

"I'll be waiting at the airport for you when you land," Norah promised eagerly.

SHE MET HIS PLANE four hours later. Rowdy was the first one to disembark and he walked out of the jetway and directly to Norah. They just stood there for an instant, staring at each other, before he sighed and pulled her into his embrace.

"Damn fool woman," he muttered, then he kissed her hungrily.

"Who, me or Valerie?" she asked, wrapping her arms around his neck. He'd lifted her clear off the floor, leaving her feet dangling.

"Both of you."

"Love isn't a business deal, Rowdy. It's you and me settling our differences. I don't ever want to go through this again."

"You?" he cried, and buried his face in her neck. "I don't think my heart could bear it." He laughed shakily. "Until I met you, Norah Bloomfield, I didn't even know I had a heart."

Gradually he lowered her back to the floor. His eyes, so loving and intense, continued to hold hers. "I thought I'd go crazy the past couple of days," he admitted. "So did everyone around me. Mrs. Emerich was so furious with me that she threatened to resign."

"She really is a dear."

Rowdy chuckled. "Maybe, but I advise you not to make her angry."

Norah laughed softly and slipped her arm around his waist. "What changed your mind?"

Rowdy kissed the top of her head. "Something you said a long time back."

"Something I said?"

He nodded and kissed her cheek. "About what's really important in life. You said love and fulfillment came from people and relationships. I was sitting at my desk last night, and I realized I was working myself to death for no good reason. I was filling up all the emptiness I've felt in my life with business. What I really wanted was you. I wanted you to lecture me about my cholesterol count. I wanted you to argue with me about what we're going to name our children and where we're going to spend our vacations. I wanted you to kiss me."

"Oh, Rowdy." Tears filled her eyes until his precious face blurred before her.

"Damn, but I'm crazy about you." He drew her into his arms again. "Let's start with the kissing part," he whispered.

Norah smiled through her tears. "That's one thing I won't argue about."

EPILOGUE

"OH, ROWDY, I'm so anxious to see my family," Norah breathed as she settled into the airplane beside her husband. She didn't know if she'd ever grow accustomed to flying in the small jet Rowdy kept for personal use, but it was a definite convenience since the Lear could land at the tiny Orchard Valley airport.

"I don't know why Valerie had to plan a big reunion three weeks before your due date," Rowdy returned, glancing anxiously at Norah's swollen abdomen. A toddler slept in his arms, head resting on Rowdy's broad shoulder. Rowdy lovingly held his hand against his son's back.

"Don't fuss. She planned this get-together a year ago, before we knew about the baby."

"I still don't think you should be traveling."

Norah smiled reassuringly at her husband. "We couldn't be in finer company. If the baby does decide to arrive early, Colby will be there to help with the delivery. Besides, Jeff arrived a week late."

"There's nothing to say this baby might come early," Rowdy argued. "Anyway, Colby's a heart surgeon."

"He knows everything there is to know about babies," Norah countered, smiling softly to herself. She never would have believed Rowdy would fret so much over her pregnancies. He was fiercely protective when it came to Norah and their family.

For the first time since they entered the aircraft, Rowdy grinned. "Colby certainly *should* know about babies. Even now, it's difficult for me to picture Valerie as the mother of twins."

"Valerie amazes me," Norah said, with a genuine sigh of admiration. Her eldest sister continued to head CHIPS Northwest, cared for both her sons and accomplished more in one day than Norah thought about doing in a week. Her family and CHIPS both thrived.

Rowdy's eyes softened as they met Norah's. "*You* amaze me."

"I do?"

If there'd been any surprises in her marriage, they had come from the changes she'd seen in Rowdy. No wife could ask for a more attentive husband. He'd learned to delegate duties, and CHIPS was now served by four vice presidents. He'd promoted Valerie almost immediately after she'd agreed to accept the Northwest position.

The most incredible thing had happened as Rowdy gradually released the tight control he held over every aspect of his company. CHIPS prospered. The stock had nearly doubled in the two and a half years since Norah and Rowdy's marriage.

"I have so much to thank you for," Rowdy said, tucking his arm around her shoulder and drawing her closer to him. He rested his free hand on her stomach and Norah watched his eyes widen as he felt their child kick against his palm.

"The baby moved!"

Norah laughed. "Yes, I know."

Rowdy's grin broadened. "The closer the time comes for this one to be born, the more excited I get." He kissed Jeff's blond head. "It surprises me how anyone so little could take up so much of my heart," he said solemnly.

"You're a wonderful father," Norah whispered. "And you know what else?" she asked, nestling against him. "You're a wonderful husband, too."

"You make that very easy, angel face." He settled his arm around her shoulders and Norah felt him kiss the top of her head. He rested his chin there. "I was thinking the other day that if we have a girl, we should name her Grace—after your mother."

Norah smiled softly to herself. "I'm so happy you said that."

"Does your father think baby number two will be a boy or a girl?"

Norah sighed. "Just because he was right about Valerie and Colby having twin boys, and Steffie and Charles having a little girl, that doesn't mean what he predicted for us would come true. Having six kids is probably excessive—even for us!"

Norah felt Rowdy go still. She raised her head to look into her husband's dark eyes. "You're thinking about those children again, aren't you?" she said quietly, referring to the recent, tragic death of one of his employees, who'd left two orphaned children.

Rowdy nodded. "I know what it's like to lose your mother and father. I hate the thought of those two spending the rest of their lives being shuffled from foster home to foster home the same way I was."

"You have a soft heart, Rowdy Cassidy. I have a distinct feeling we're going to end up with six children, after all."

"Would you mind?"

"I wouldn't mind in the least," she assured him.

The drone of the airplane quickly put Norah to sleep. When she awoke, it was nearly time for them to land. Steffie and Charles had volunteered to pick them up at the tiny Orchard Valley airport and drive them to the house.

Norah stepped off the plane first and was greeted with a hug from Steffie. Marriage hadn't changed her. Steffie was as graceful as a ballerina and so beautiful that it took Norah a moment to stop looking at her.

"It's so good to see you," Steffie squealed. Charles was holding a squirming toddler against his hip. "Hello, Amy," Norah said, holding out her arms to her ten-month-old niece. "Do you remember your Auntie Norah?"

"She might," Steffie teased, "but I don't think she's so sure about the tummy."

"She's far more interested in reacquainting herself with Jeff," Charles suggested as the two cousins eyed each other.

"How's Dad?" Norah asked as they walked toward the car.

"Never better," Charles answered. "He's so excited about this family get-together that he can hardly stand it. I swear he must have been up before the crack of dawn this morning. Wait until you see the spread he's arranged. The front yard is all ready for the barbecue."

"Dad's turned into a professional Grandpa," Steffie put in. "He's wonderful with Amy and the boys. I never thought I'd see Dad down on his hands and knees giving horsey rides. Trust me, it's a sight to behold."

Norah grinned. It seemed impossible that a few short years ago she'd been convinced they would lose him. He'd lost the will to live and given up the struggle to regain his health.

They talked at least once a week on the phone, and sometimes more often. Her father loved to fill her in on the Orchard Valley news. Since Charles was the local newspaper's publisher and editor, David had an inside track on the town's affairs. It seemed something was always going on. Their weekly calls had helped Norah those first weeks, when she'd missed home so much....

DAVID BLOOMFIELD was standing on the front porch, waiting for his family to arrive. When Rowdy helped Norah out of the car, he saw the gruff cowboy watching her tenderly as he carried their young son. Charles and Steffie and little Amy appeared next. David saw the gentle communication between his second daughter and her husband, saw how proud Steffie was of him and how deeply they loved their child.

Valerie and Colby, who'd been occupied playing with their identical twin sons on the swing set, waved and shouted a cheer of welcome. The two boys took off running toward the parked car, laughing, their eyes shining with joy. Hand in hand, Valerie and Colby followed them. The children's peals of laughter rippled through the early afternoon air, and David grinned. His heart swelled at the sight of his three daughters and their families. Valerie and Colby with the twins, Steffie and Charles with their little girl, and Norah with her son and another one due within the month.

"It's just the way you said it would be," David said hoarsely, looking to the heavens. "More than I ever dreamed it would be." He wiped a stray tear from his eye and whispered, "Thank you, Grace."

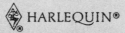

The most romantic day of the year is here! Escape into the exquisite world of love with MY VALENTINE 1993. What better way to celebrate Valentine's Day than with this very romantic, sensuous collection of four original short stories, written by some of Harlequin's most popular authors.

ANNE STUART
JUDITH ARNOLD
ANNE McALLISTER
LINDA RANDALL WISDOM

THIS VALENTINE'S DAY, DISCOVER ROMANCE
WITH MY VALENTINE 1993

Available in February wherever Harlequin Books are sold.   VAL93

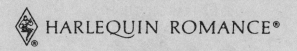

HARLEQUIN ROMANCE®

Norah Bloomfield's father is recovering from his heart attack, and her sisters are getting married. So Norah's feeling a bit unneeded these days, a bit left out....

Orchard Valley

And then a cantankerous "cowboy" called Rowdy Cassidy crashes into her life!

"The Orchard Valley trilogy features three delightful, spirited sisters and a trio of equally fascinating men. The stories are rich with the romance, warmth of heart and humor readers expect, and invariably receive, from Debbie Macomber."

—Linda Lael Miller

Don't miss the Orchard Valley trilogy by Debbie Macomber:

VALERIE Harlequin Romance #3232 (November 1992)
STEPHANIE Harlequin Romance #3239 (December 1992)
NORAH Harlequin Romance #3244 (January 1993)

Look for the special cover flash on each book!

Available wherever Harlequin books are sold. ORC-3

COME FOR A VISIT—TEXAS-STYLE!

Where do you find hot Texas nights, smooth Texas charm and dangerously sexy cowboys? CRYSTAL CREEK!

This March, join us for a year in Crystal Creek...where power and influence live in the land, and in the hands of one family determined to nourish old Texas fortunes and to forge new Texas futures.

CRYSTAL CREEK reverberates with the exciting rhythm of Texas. Each story features the rugged individuals who live and love in the Lone Star State. And each one ends with the same invitation...

Y'ALL COME BACK...REAL SOON!

Watch for this exciting saga of a unique Texas family in March, wherever Harlequin Books are sold.

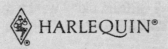

HARLEQUIN ROMANCE®

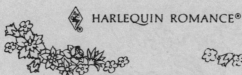

**Harlequin Romance
takes you to Alaska
for a wedding!**

Join us there
when you read
next month's title in

THE BRIDAL COLLECTION

A BRIDE FOR RANSOM (#3251)
by Renee Roszel

THE BRIDE wasn't looking for a husband.
THE GROOM didn't want a wife.
BUT THE WEDDING was right for both of them!

Available this month in
The Bridal Collection:
SHOWDOWN!
by Ruth Jean Dale
Harlequin Romance #3242

WED-10